The Ultimate Dinosaur Dance-Off

ANDREW J. STONE

Copyright © Andrew J. Stone

All rights reserved. No part of this book may be reproduced or transmitted in any form or by any means, electronic or mechanical, including photocopying, recording, or by any information storage and retrieval system, without the written consent of the publisher, except where permitted by law.

ISBN:978-1-950305-37-7 (sc)
ISBN:978-1-950305-38-4 (ebook)

First printing edition: September 28, 2020
Published by Bizarro Pulp Press in the United States of America.
Cover Design by Nicholas Day and Don Noble
Layout/Interior Layout Don Noble
Edited by Nicholas Day

Bizarro Pulp Press, an imprint of JournalStone Publishing
3205 Sassafras Trail
Carbondale, Illinois 62901

Bizarro Pulp Press may be ordered through booksellers or by contacting:
JournalStone | www.journalstone.com

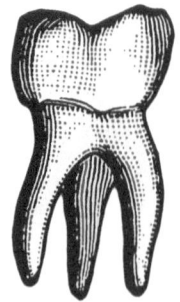

"*The Ultimate Dinosaur Dance-Off* is a cavalcade of daft, enjoyable fun. When the whole planet is drowning in seriousness sometimes it's necessary to escape into a world of Tyrannosaurus Task Forces, deadly dance moves, and anal parrots."

– Madeleine Swann, author of *Fortune Box*

"Andrew Stone's *The Ultimate Dinosaur Dance-Off* has one of the strangest premises ever put on paper—a universe of ancient animals on shifting planes of existence whose driving force is getting footloose and a showdown of epic proportions in an otherworldly, apocalyptic discotheque. It's a lot of madness to hang together, but Stone keeps the action hopping along at a boogaloo pace, and the story's weird trappings are rooted in the emotional longing at its core.

"The strangest love story ever told" was the tagline of the 1931 film of *Dracula*, but it's better applied here, as Stone generates real romantic sparks between two of his characters, only one of which is human. The overall effect is more lighthearted than most other Bizarro I've read, as the story mostly avoids violence and instead strikes a tone of humorous adventure—an uplifting read in these strange times we live in, which don't seem so strange when compared to this book."

–Andrew Goldfarb, author of *Midnight Earwig Buffet* and the lone member of the psychedelic rock band The Slow Poisoner

Praise for *The Mortuary Monster*:

"The only book in recent memory that I read, then immediately reread, then have kept peeking back at ever since, just to make sure it didn't change into something else when I wasn't looking. As deeply abnormal a narrative as you are ever likely to find, with a monster I would beat to death if I weren't so fucking sad. Awfully wonderful, and beautifully wrong. I would play baseball with *The Mortuary Monster*, and you should, too. Just watch out for the ankle violence!"

—John Skipp, author of *The Light at the End* and *The Art of Horrible People*

Praise for *All Hail the House Gods*:

"Fans of the bizarre and the grotesque will find plenty to enjoy in Andrew Stone's writing, but they may also find something that surprises them: a warmth; a humanity; an inventive way with language that makes the weirdness all the more persuasive. The Stone universe is too unsettling a place for most of us to feel comfortable for very long but it's a remarkably, deceptively hospitable place to visit."

—Geoff Nicholson, author of *Bleeding London and The Miranda*

"What is the use of protest? What is the purpose of fighting injustice against powers that lure you with the smell of scented candles, high ceilings, and unquestionable superiority in strength? Death is assured.

And yet... as our hero in *All Hail the House Gods* awaits his ultimate sacrifice, he recounts a story of the power of the failed, doomed, and vital relationships in his rise against the Almighty structures.

A joy-ride of a read, Stone has created a compelling morality tale that's moral lies somewhere in tomorrow's déjà vu. Funny, sad, stunning in its imaginative realization, Andrew J. Stone's new novel is as topical, timely, and telling as a Freudian slip."

—Laura Lee Bahr, author of *Haunt* and *Angel Meat*

"Andrew Stone writes like a laser beam shot out of a unicorn horn. His books will alter your brain in the best possible way. If an LSD Bible had babies with a hand grenade poetry collection, you'd get what Stone can do. He's dazzling."

—Brian Allen Carr, author of *Sip and Motherfucking Sharks*

"*All Hail the House Gods* doesn't just savagely reboot the dystopian novel with surreal flair. It strips away the most fundamentally received truths about how we live and what we live for. Truly an author to watch out for, in the most cautionary sense. Seriously, if you let him in your head, he'll wreck the place."

–Cody Goodfellow, Wonderland Award-winning author of *Sleazeland* and *All-Monster Action*

"In *All Hail the House Gods*, Andrew J. Stone has created an unsettling and terrifying alternate dimension where procreation is the ultimate patriotic duty. The writing is satirical, sinister, and unafraid to explore the uncomfortable realities of humanity. The story poses questions regarding sexual bodily autonomy and what happens when this is taken away and turned into a mechanism of self-sacrifice for your country. Stone uses gorgeous, psychedelic, and hilarious imagery to move you further and further into this world where the powerless begin to explore methods of rebellion against a power structure that kills them one by one."

–Rios de la Luz, author of *Itzá*

To Lindsey, without whom none of this would be possible.
To Wesley and Magnolia, the lights of my life.
And to Apatosauruses, the coolest fucking creatures to have ever
roamed the Earth.

THE *JOLLY DANCER* (CHAPTER ONE)

COLIN DANCED. He did not usually dance in front of his friends, but as he shook his hips from side to side and waved his hands above his head, he felt slightly less awkward than he would have imagined. Generally, he only danced when he knew people weren't watching. He danced every morning while he showered, every afternoon as he stared at the dinosaur art in his campus apartment, and every evening as he heated a frozen dinner. Even though he usually danced alone, he secretly dreamed to captain the best competitive dance team in the world. But that would require him to study dance in addition to geology, which, as his father had repeatedly insisted, did not align with Colin's best interest. In fear of losing his financial support, Colin had kept his dancing in the closet. But tonight at the campground, under the influence of T. Rex's "Cosmic Dancer," the desire to dance seized control of his body. Across the campfire, Colin saw his twin brother, Joe, and Emma, Joe's girlfriend, mirroring his movements as if they were shadows swaying in smoke.

As Colin envisioned his crew solving his life's problems through the power of unified dance, a strange light illuminated the face of the Big Four Ice Caves just beyond the edge of their campsite. The cold glow slowly shifted from shades of green to shades of purple, from purple to blue, and blue back to green.

And over the climax of "Cosmic Dancer," Emma shouted, "Do you guys see that light, too?"

"Yeah," Joe said, his dance stiffening into a stance. "Let's check it out."

Joe wrapped an arm around Emma, and their bodies carried them toward the luminescence. As Colin watched them go, he wished they would come back to the comfort of the campfire. He wanted to get lost in the movement of the music again. He wanted to dream of leading them to dance-off glory. But most of all, he didn't want to waste this chance to dance by investigating the light emitting from the ice caves.

By the time Joe and Emma had walked the length of a roller disco rink, covering half the distance to the caves, Colin's stubbornness had started to subside. When he moved away from the tent toward them, the warmth of the campfire crawled down his back. It bled into the wet dirt below his feet, and as the cold grew, the sounds of the song scattered like ash.

"Do you think it's safe?" Colin asked as he reached the entrance to the ice caves.

"Does it matter?" asked Joe.

Colin trailed his twin brother and Emma into one of the caves, and its cold body began to morph around them. The mouth grew icicle teeth, and the dirt-stained snow turned to algae-colored scales. Deeper in the ice cave the cadaverine and putrescine coalesced—as if they had crept into the carcass of a decaying dinosaur. When they reached the end of the tunnel, the snow around them began to whirlpool, and before Colin understood what happened, the slush beneath them started to swirl and flushed them into the cave's underground cavern.

Colin landed on his back in a pile of powder. He raised himself out of the cold and shook it off his clothes, leaving behind the imprint of a snow skeleton. He watched his brother and Emma walk before him, their bodies nothing more than silhouettes fading into the source of the colorful light. As he went after them, he realized icicles had grown out of the white ground, curving into an arch above him. They reminded Colin of Sue's ribcage: the biggest Tyrannosaurus Rex fossil ever found, which he saw in Chicago as a child when he and his brother vacationed with their dad. Colin had been obsessed with dinosaurs ever since. And as a result of his *unhealthy* adoration, the icicle dinosaur bones transfixed Colin so completely that he didn't realize Joe and Emma had stopped, and he walked straight into them.

"Look," Joe said to Colin, pointing toward the color.

After a few seconds, Colin's eyes adjusted to the intense light. At the end of the archway, in the pit of the Tyrannosaurus Rex's skeletal stomach, stood a massive pirate ship. The ship's color scheme constantly shifted between tie-dye shades of green, purple, and blue. On its side, neon orange letters declaring the *Jolly Dancer* had started to decay. MC Hammer's "U Can't Touch This" began to radiate from the ship, and Joe and Emma started to gravitate toward the front of the brig. Colin followed. Once he stood before the bow, he stared at the long-necked figurehead.

"Is this ship a... dinosaur?" Colin asked, stunned.

"Yeah man," Joe said. "I think so."

"Of course I'm a dinosaur," declared the ship. Its voice reminded Colin of a parrot, and as it spoke, he realized that the figurehead existed as more than just an eccentric decoration. The longneck dinosaur and the pirate ship morphed into a cohesive being, and the body of the brig became more and more abdominal.

Colin had spent his entire life wanting nothing more than to meet a dinosaur, but now that he stood a few feet from one, he couldn't bring himself to act. His body trembled, and he couldn't help but envision himself on a date with the dinosaur, sailing this ship through Mesozoic seas. Even though the longneck looked as if it were made of real flesh and the rest of the ship had taken on a reptilian quality, Colin fully believed the whole ship consisted of wood. Regardless of the dinosaur's legitimacy, he told himself to remain calm. He didn't want to scare the ship, or worse, annoy it.

"Colin!" Joe shouted.

Before he could respond, he noticed that Joe and Emma were cha-cha-chaing through the air toward the ship. Colin tried to ask them how they were floating, but the louder he shouted, the quieter his voice became, until the words leaving his lips were simply susurrus.

"Dance," Emma said, her command cutting clearly through MC Hammer's song. Not knowing what dance to do, Colin acted on the first impulse that came, and he performed the most powerful and moving sprinkler of his life. Before Colin had the chance to bring his arm back around, his feet had left the ground.

"It's working," Colin said, as the power of the sprinkler carried him through the air toward the pirate ship.

"Of course it's working," the ship said. "I'm the *Jolly Dancer.* I'm powered by the spirit of dance. Dance brings you to board me, dance brings me to make music, and dance will lift me off the ground."

Emma danced a stationary mutation of the Texas two-step with an invisible partner and Joe did the worm as Colin's feet touched the ship's surface. He had no idea what dance he could do that would match the talent of the two of them. He wished he could feel the way he did when he danced in the shower—god-like and proud. But as he stood there on the ship, his once powerful sprinkler dripped water as if he were a defunct faucet. Colin felt unworthy, wimpy.

Somehow he managed to find the courage to ask, "What do we do now?"

"Now," the longneck figurehead said, "you break it down."

Then, as if some unseen force had usurped Colin's body, he began to do the running man. As he looked to his left and his right, he saw that Joe and Emma had joined him in his dance. Simultaneously, the three of them shuffled their feet. And under the guidance of the longneck, the ship shook violently, causing Colin to fall to the floor.

"What was that?" Colin asked, lifting himself back to his feet. And without missing a beat, he continued to dance.

"Your dancing has dislodged me from the snow," the ship shouted as it began to float. "We'll be out of here in no time."

Colin shuffled to the side of the ship and peeked over its edge. Despite the massive quake and the longneck's words, and despite being on a brightly lit color-shifting pirate ship beneath an ice cave, that the vessel indeed floated surprised Colin. When he first looked, only a couple of feet separated the ship from the floor. But it rose quickly, and within a few seconds it had floated at least three times as high.

Suddenly, giant icicles crashed down onto the ship. Colin's body shivered as he hesitantly shuffled his way back between Joe and Emma, weaving through the snow spears.

Colin continued to dodge the cascading icicles as his group grooved to the music, and the Tyrannosaurus Rex ice cave expelled a resounding burp. The longneck figurehead said, "You need to dance your way out of this cave or the ice will crush you!"

"There's no way out," Colin said.

"He's right," Emma said, her eyes scanning the entirety of the ice cave's interior. "We're trapped."

"Trust me, there's a way," the ship said. "As you run in place, spin your bodies counterclockwise."

The dancers did as they were told, and the ship shot upwards, toward the roof of the ice cave's cavern. The brig broke through the snowy ground, puncturing the fossilized Tyrannosaurus Rex's uvula in the process, causing it to regurgitate. The Tyrannosaurus Rex ice cave vomited so hard that it propelled the ship toward space.

"Holy fuck," Colin said, as they passed through a cloud. "We're flying!"

"Of course we're flying," the ship said. "How else would we get to the Black Hole of the Brontosaurus?"

"The Black Hole of the what?" Emma asked.

"Brontosaurus," Colin said. "It's a dinosaur. But no one is really sure if it's real or not."

"Is that where you're taking us?" Joe asked.

"No," the ship said. "As long as all of you keep dancing, that's where you're taking me."

And as they broke through the exosphere into outer space, "Cosmic Dancer" came from the belly of the brig. Subconsciously, Colin's shuffle changed to an awkward moonwalk. He looked toward Joe and Emma and saw that they were doing the moonwalk, too. Albeit, their choreography looked much more convincing.

The ship carried them past the moon and stars, which were as big as ballrooms. Despite his awe, Colin couldn't deny his exhaustion, and a long yawn escaped his lips as the ship hurtled deeper into the darkness.

Colin slapped himself in the face. He tried to imagine being fellated by a sauropod, his favorite order of dinosaurs, to keep himself awake so he could continue to moonwalk the ship toward the Black Hole of the Brontosaurus.

Black Hole of the Brontosaurus (Chapter Two)

COLIN GLANCED BACK at Earth as he danced the pirate ship through space. His planet looked like a miniature ocean-blue island in a vast sea of starry darkness.

"We're pretty far out," he said. "Ready to call it a night?"

"Fuck that," Joe said, rubbing his hands together, reviving his fingers with warm exhalations. "We have to see the Black Hole of the Brontosaurus."

"Yeah," Emma agreed, her pointed chin and wide forehead shaping her face like a heart. "If we go to sleep now, we'll just wake up back at the ice caves. We have to dance a little bit longer to see where this flight takes us. And once we land the ship, you can sleep."

"That could take hours," Colin complained, "and the ship is starting to freeze." Colin slipped on the icy surface, scraping a layer of skin off his elbow.

"We can't quit now," Joe said, bending over to help up his brother. "As long as we keep dancing, the *Jolly Dancer* will see us through."

Colin sighed and cautiously resumed his moonwalk.

"If mom were still alive," Joe said, nodding his head to the music as he danced, "I bet she'd be proud."

"Bullshit." Colin's moonwalk tapered off to a grounded glide.

"After all these years, she'd be stoked that you're finally

dancing." Joe's eyes were closed. He seemed mesmerized by the interaction between the music and his movement.

"I doubt she'd be proud of this."

"You're not that bad," Joe said, eyes still shut.

"I'd be a lot better if I could lie to dad like you. Maybe I'd study dance in addition to geology."

"Or if you had just danced," Emma said.

"I couldn't," Colin said, annoyed.

"Or what? Your shit dad might disown you like he did Joe?" Emma asked.

"At least there's a future in geology," Joe said, changing the subject. "Emma and I could be the best damn dancers in the world, but that still doesn't guarantee us anything post-graduation. Plus, we don't know shit about science, while you don't completely suck at dancing."

"There's no future for me," Colin said. "I just wish I could dance."

Sick of the cold and tired of sliding his feet, Colin prepared to call it quits. But just before he fell to the floor and rested his head in his arms, the stars straight ahead imploded with color. Pockets of pink, purple, blue, green, and gold spread through outer space, outlining the shape of an animal.

"Look at that," Emma said, as the ship steadily carried them closer. "It's beautiful."

"What is it?" Joe asked, opening his eyes.

"It's the Black Hole of the Brontosaurus," Colin said, elated.

"Are you sure?" Joe asked.

"No," Colin said, "but the stars outline the body of a Brontosaurus. And see the small space in the color where the darkness shines? I bet that's where we're heading."

Approaching the black hole rejuvenated Colin. Dancing no longer felt like a chore, but without exhaustion to distract him, he realized how stupid he looked. Colin glanced at his brother for guidance, but all he saw was the dancer he would never be.

Colin looked overboard, and one of the stars morphed into the face of his father. The star said, "Son, I see you dancing."

"You're just a star," Colin said.

"I may be," the star said. "But I'm a star that can cut off your income and leave you on the streets after you graduate."

"But it's the only way to discover dinosaurs, dad. Think of

how much this could help your art career to depict them literally?"

"I don't give a shit what dinosaurs look like," the star said. "All I care about if your safety. After losing your mother and brother to dance, I cannot bear of the thought of losing you. Stop dancing and come home."

"Joe's still here, in case you forgot," Colin said.

"No thanks to dance," the star said. "It nearly killed him, too, and I can't go through that shit again. It's why he left me no choice. And why you'll leave me no choice, Colin, if you continue down this horrible path."

Before Colin could respond, his father's face faded from the star. In order to forget his father, Colin dreamed of Apatosauruses. In order to keep fueling the ship with his miserable moonwalk, Colin directed his gaze at the cosmic dinosaur. Even then, when they finally reached the Brontosaurus's dark spot, Colin's cheeks burned as if he had swallowed the sun.

The black hole sucked in the ship, and The Move's "Brontosaurus" blared from the brig. The dancing trio's moonwalk shifted to a slow and sultry electric slide.

The ship dipped after entering the black hole, causing Colin's stomach to act as if it were springing out of his body. But once the gravitational force settled and Colin's stomach returned, he discovered that humid heat had replaced the cold of the cosmos, which caused his nerves to flare. The heat continued to rise, thinning the ice surrounding the ship's surface. As they sailed further into the black hole, the color of the Brontosaurus's starry body started to shoot through the darkness. As the song picked up its pace, approaching its climax, Colin accelerated his electric slide, dancing the ship into light speed as they crossed through the Brontosaurus's rainbow body. The sudden increase of velocity caused Colin to retch, and the figurehead tweaked its neck, unknotting a crick with a loud crack.

The longneck let out a lengthy sigh before it stretched and turned to face Colin and the others. "The Black Hole of the Brontosaurus is sending us through space and time to the Days of the Dinosaur. Just keep dancing and we'll be there before you can blink."

"The Days of the Dinosaur," Colin whispered, awed. He

blinked as rapidly as possible, but no matter how quickly he operated his eyelids, the dinosaur island refused to surface.

As they progressed through the portal, Colin added more and more vigor to his moves, exaggerating his electric slide as if he were creating craters in time by dragging his feet. He wondered what the dinosaurs would look like, if they'd fit the mold of modern science, feathers and all, or if they'd be closer to the paleoart his dad made, influenced by pop culture and cinema. And the strength with which he slid his feet consistently increased until the heat and humidity started to suffocate him, causing him to feel curiously claustrophobic.

A bright beam of clear yellow light eventually broke through the rainbow. Colin closed his eyes as the ship sailed into sunshine.

And before his vision could adjust to the strong rays of light on the other side of his hands, the ship plummeted into a prehistoric pasture, shattering the wood of the hull as if it were a dinosaur fossil they had danced into dynamite.

BEFORE THE VOYAGE (CHAPTER THREE)

COLIN'S TRIP TO THE BIG FOUR ICE CAVES almost didn't happen. Not because he had to convince anyone to go camping with him the weekend before their last college finals, but because he came up with the idea for the trip, and consequently, he had to plan it.

The idea for the trip came to Colin suddenly, after he received a rejection regarding his last pending application to a graduate paleontology program. Before this letter, Colin had somehow succeeded in convincing himself that all his other rejections were a good thing because it meant that once he got into his dream school, he wouldn't have any competing offers, one of which might have been impossible to forgo. Ergo, fate had been opening the door to his dream school all along. Despite his self-deception, the day he finally received an envelope bearing the University of Chicago's emblem, Colin couldn't contain his anxiety. Once he held the holy mail in his hands, he rushed to his room and locked the door, trembling the entire time. He set the prized paper on his desk and retrieved his cosmic dinosaur sweater from the closet. And only after Colin lay comfortably atop his comforter and wore his lucky sweater did he reach for the envelope on the desk beside his bed.

Slowly, like a heart surgeon, Colin slit the seal of the envelope. He had one eye shut as he extracted the letter, and it remained closed until he had finished unfolding the paper. And after he read the first sentence, Colin learned that fate was a fucking liar.

Without the research privileges a paleontology degree presented, Colin would never be able to hold dinosaur bones in his hands, would never have the freedom to spend time alone with actual sauropod fossils all around the world. To avoid focusing on his crushed dreams, thereby keeping the water in his eyes, Colin decided that next weekend he and his housemates would go on a camping trip to dance away the depression and disappointment.

After an hour of unsuccessful attempts, Colin finally found the will to lift himself out of bed and walk to his housemates' room. When he reached their door, he heard mountainous moans coming from within. Colin started to withdraw, but after retracting a few steps, thought, *screw it*, and obnoxiously knocked his knuckles against the wood. He heard his brother and Emma scrambling around, hissing at one another, until a moment later one of them unlatched the lock. Shocking Blue's "Love Buzz" bled into the hall.

Joe peeked his head out the door, which hid his body in darkness. "Hey Colin," he said, "what do you want?"

"This weekend," Colin said, "let's go camping at the Big Four Ice Caves."

"I don't know," Joe said. "Emma and I have the biggest performance of our lives coming up for our finals."

"But this is the last of our trifecta of camping trips before we graduate. We're so close. We can't quit now. Besides, I could really use the brief break to space out and avoid the shit going down here. Please?"

Joe sighed. Skeptically, he asked, "You making all the plans? Emma and I don't have any time for preparations. We'll be rehearsing our dances all week. If we fuck this up and lose our full-rides to CalArts, we'll be couch surfing come graduation."

"Yeah," Colin said, scratching the side of his neck, "sure."

"In that case, if it will get you to leave us alone, then we'd love to go."

"Great," Colin said, the door slamming into his face.

Before he began to retrace his steps back to his room, he heard the springs quiver. And for the rest of the night, he avoided studying by lying under the sheets and listening to Joe and

17

Emma. Just before drifting off to sleep, he looked at a piece of paleoart hanging on his wall. The painting depicted his favorite dinosaur, the long-necked Apatosaurus. He placed a hand inside his pajama pants and hypothesized different ways sauropods could have fucked.

—

Throughout the week, Colin avoided piecing the trip together, electing to hang out with friends in his geology program instead. He justified this decision by telling himself that when he got home from the bars, he'd study for his finals, and after that, he'd plan the camping trip. In actuality, he just went to bars with his friends, listened to their beverage-enhanced boasts of all the cool shit fate had in store for them post-graduation, while he sat in silence, drowning his brain. After he managed to stumble back to his apartment, he flopped into bed, instantly passing into unconsciousness.

Colin followed this routine till Thursday, the night before he, his brother, and Emma had planned to leave for their trip. Despite his best efforts to avoid school all week with friends, he couldn't convince any of them to hit up some bars that night. They all gave him the same excuse: They were studying for finals. As a result, he decided he would begin to piece the camping trip together. A couple of hours later, he had everything arranged.

The hour had turned late enough for Colin to replace the possibility of studying with sleep. He placed *Environmental Geology* under his pillow, but before he went to bed, he left his room to inform Joe and Emma that the plans had been made. They would be leaving for the Big Four Ice Caves first thing tomorrow afternoon.

Dancing with Dinosaurs (Chapter Four)

NEITHER COLIN, JOE NOR EMMA were injured by the *Jolly Dancer's* destructive descent into prehistoric times, but it seemed the ship had sustained irrevocable damage. The longneck figurehead had become completely severed from its body, in addition to being split in half. Moreover, the brig itself consisted of nothing but a few thousand splinters splayed throughout the crystallized grass. The Move's "Brontosaurus" had sunk with the ship, and in this silence, Colin's electric slide transitioned to a shuffle. He danced toward the tree line as fast as humanly possible, scuttling away from the island's cliff. He kept seeing his father's artistic depictions of dinosaurs, but as his excitement expanded, the images of the paleoart became lost, and his imagination grew increasingly colorful and cloudy.

As Colin approached the halfway point to the rainbow forest, he shuffled under a leaning archway, which had one leg significantly shorter than the other. Across the top, in neon orange scribbles, it announced that he had reached the Days of the Dinosaur. He looked back to Joe and Emma, sporting a smile like a pirate ship as he envisioned himself riding a sauropod. But the two of them were still electric sliding before the remains of the wooden Brontosaurus.

Colin shouted, "Who cares about the ship? We're about to see real dinosaurs!"

Joe looked up, sliding sadly, "But how will we get home?"

"And what about our finals?" Emma added as woodchips sifted through her fingers. "What if we can't graduate?"

Colin shrugged. He wished his housemates understood the magnitude of this moment. Couldn't they see that they were about to do something no other human had done before? That they were about to make contact with dinosaurs?

On the other side of the sign, the pasture continued for a couple of hundred yards or so before giving way to a dense forest. As Colin gyrated past the archway, he noted that the vibes of the atmosphere had altered. He thought the crystallized grass beneath his feet smiled and waved to him. Overhead, the sky dripped shades of rainbow sherbet, and the heat had skyrocketed past any climate Colin knew in the history of his life. The humidity clung to his skin like a leech.

Colin's brother and his girlfriend caught up with Colin seconds before he shuffled his way into the forest, and as they danced together, dinosaurs bloomed from the bushes. Nine of them appeared—their skin sharing the same vibrant green, purple, and blue tie-dye hues as the *Jolly Dancer*—and the moment they arrived, the dinosaurs started to shimmy. They rhythmically whipped their necks and tails from side to side, grooving on their four herculean, pillar-like legs while Colin pinched the lobes of his ear. As his nails bit into his soft flesh, he stared at the dinosaurs in disbelief. He danced in the presence of genuine Apatosauruses.

Disregarding all style and rhythm, Colin joined the dinosaurs in their dance by jumping up and down, throwing his arms above his head, and hyperventilating. He tried to coerce himself into behaving somewhat human, but despite his greatest exertion of self-control, Colin could not contain his excitement. He continued to romp around the sauropods like a raving lunatic.

Through his peripheral vision, Colin noticed that Joe and Emma had joined the dancing dinosaurs, too, though the dinosaurs had enchanted Colin so completely that Joe and Emma's ability to blend their movements with those of the Apatosauruses no longer distressed him in the slightest. Hypnotized by his childhood dream coming to life, he just kept flailing his body like a floundering fish.

The Apatosauruses' sensuous tie-dye skin, as opposed to

looking like a scaly swamp, did not shock Colin. The dinosaurs' dancing, as opposed to eating, sleeping, or copulating, did not confuse him either. But the lack of song had taken Colin wholly by surprise. And as if this thought had triggered something in the prehistoric universe, Jefferson Airplane's "We Can Be Together" replaced the sounds of meat slapping air, the animal grunts of humans and dinosaurs as they grooved together.

The addition of Jefferson Airplane to the already celestial scene proved to be too much for Colin. As the chorus of the song chimed, he mistakenly took the Apatosauruses' sublime state to be the result of his dancing. Colin had become so captivated by the moment that he convinced himself the dinosaurs looked transcendent because, after witnessing his ability to dance, they believed they should all be together.

But his delusions were quickly squashed. As the song came down from its initial chorus, Colin returned to reality long enough to realize that he had not, in fact, mastered the art of dance. All too abruptly, Colin became aware that among the humans and the Apatosauruses, he remained the only being who had absolutely no knack for dancing. His cheeks glowed red, and because of the burning embarrassment, he did something he had never done before: Colin swore that he would do whatever it took to significantly improve his ability to dance. Of course, he had made plenty of self-promises in the past. But what differentiated this pledge was that he made it while believing the impossible.

Colin didn't have to wait long before he could start keeping his covenant, either. As the chorus rolled around again, the Apatosauruses paired off with each other, leaving one of the dinosaurs, the most colorful of the sauropods, without a dance partner. Emma and Joe paired off, too, so Colin remained the only candidate to dance with the dinosaur. Timidly, he trudged forward. Once he came within a foot of contact, the Apatosaurus bent her burly neck so he could take her head in his left hand, and she tipped her willowy tail so he could hold it with his right. Her scent reminded him of amber incense, and his stomach fluttered. Once their limbs enlaced, Colin chewed the inside of his lower lip. He tasted blood, felt pain, before the jittery euphoria of being intertwined with this dinosaur enveloped him. The Apatosaurus led Colin in the psychedelic swing.

He followed the dinosaur's movements, slowly shifting his weight from foot to foot, joyously kicking them into the air. Each time he stretched his leg he saw it span for miles, spiraling into strange angles that he thought must be irreversible, and he worried that he'd never see his feet again. But the second he brought a leg back toward the crystallized grass, it shrank to its normal size.

After a series of leg movements, the Apatosaurus used her head to knock him toward her tail. Colin felt his descent had lasted for hours before the dinosaur's tail wrapped around him and flipped him over her body. And once he landed on the other side of the Apatosaurus, she immediately flipped him over her gut again. The dinosaur then coiled her tail around Colin so she could lasso him. As the dinosaur swung him around her body, he watched the other Apatosauruses swing their partners, too. He even saw Joe lassoing Emma, his brother's left arm bonelessly circling around her feet.

The psychedelic swing was just a slightly slower paced, psychedelic version of the Lindy hop. Even then, the way the Apatosaurus led Colin in this nauseating dance convinced him that not only had Rose revealed to him the most spectacular thing to have ever happened to himself, but also to humanity and the art of dance.

The music moved into the chorus for the last time, and Colin closed his eyes so his appendages would no longer distract him. He assumed his thoughts would be about how amazing it had been to lace his limbs with a colorful Apatosaurus. He had planned on preserving every detail of his dance with the dinosaur. But when he tried to imagine the psychedelic swing, he could only picture sex. He tried to brush off the idea, reminding himself that, anatomically speaking, he didn't know how intercourse with an Apatosaurus would actually work. Though once the thought arose, he couldn't escape its visuals, never mind their accuracy. He wanted to fuck this dinosaur more than anything in the world. And after he had let this thought envelop him, it dawned on Colin that he loved this Apatosaurus, this magnificent dancing dinosaur, and he didn't even know her name.

As the song came to a close, their psychedelic swing morphed into a slow dance. And once the song had faded into complete silence, Colin heard his heart beating against the dinosaur's body through his chest. He wondered if the dinosaur could feel his palpitations.

He wished the Apatosaurus would lead him in this intimate dance until death, but eventually, and against his will, he relapsed into exhaustion. Colin succumbed to the sinking sun as he and the dinosaur slow danced themselves to sleep.

The Museum of Colin's Collected Dinosaur Art (Chapter Five)

OLIN HAD A CRUSH ON TRACEY. He noticed her the second he sat in his first college class—Introduction to Geology—and although he couldn't explain the sensation, he knew that she possessed something special. For the next couple of hours he stared at her long, red hair bobbing along her back whenever she appreciated something the teacher had said. He watched her hair for two agonizing weeks before he gathered the courage to approach. And after he introduced himself, he learned that she also studied geology as a gateway to paleontology.

After this factoid, Colin announced, "I collect paleoart," and she seemed impressed. "Whatever I could fit into my luggage," he said, "I brought to school with me. I turned half of my room into a museum. Want a private tour?"

"Possibly," Tracey said. "What dinosaurs do you have on display? Do you have any hadrosaurs?"

"Yeah," Colin said, "I have some Latirhinuses. And I promise you, my duck-billed dinosaurs have some of the biggest noses ever."

"We'll see about that," Tracey said. She curled her lips and Colin wished they'd cradle his. "Take me to Dino's Diner tonight? And after that, I'll take your tour."

"But I have Statistics tonight," Colin said. "Can't we do it tomorrow?"

"Forget about Stats," Tracey said. "I want to see your duck-billed dinosaurs." She smiled. She turned away. "I'll see you tonight." She walked into the mist.

—

When Joe and Emma entered his room after dinner, they started cuddling under the covers, watching one of their obscure dance films. They had watched a movie in bed together each night since the semester started. Colin had envied his brother's first-day fling, and his jealousy grew in correlation to their relationship. Tonight he hoped he would find his Emma.

Sheets cloaked Colin's half of the room. The sheets hung from wire that he and Joe had stuck to the ceiling, starting at the edge of the doorframe and ending against the back wall. The entrance to his homemade circus tent had been erected halfway through the room, and whenever he entered, he had to walk through what they had designated as *Joe's half of the house* in order to reach his blanket fort.

Colin led Tracey through the crack in the sheets to his bed, which awkwardly stood in the middle of his half of the room, because, as he had said, "It is the foundation of my island, and from it, you really get to experience what it would be like to live among the dinosaurs."

He put his arm around her as they lay on their backs in his bed. Tracey's front teeth peeked out from behind her lips. With his free hand he started the tour, using his finger to navigate his guest through the chaotic world of collected paleoart.

"Meet the magnificent Apatosaurus," Colin said, pointing toward the Northern half of his island, which stretched from his headboard to the dorm room's doorframe. "See the longnecks hanging their heads from heaven. See the greenery on which they graze. See their simmering scales and the smiles spread across their lips." When Colin first moved in, after he and Joe stuck his sheets to the ceiling, they drilled the necks of many different Apatosauruses to his island's sky. Their heads hung just low enough to reach the fake plants he placed along the floor between his headboard and the door. Below the plants, astroturf littered the carpeted ground. And stapled to the sheets and the walls, his father's drawings depicted what Apatosauruses must

25

have looked like based on his imagination.

Colin introduced her to the rest of the dinosaurs inhabiting the Northern Plain. "Meet the Latirhinus. See them lurking around the edge of the lake."

"They look so real," Tracey said, elated.

"Meet the Colepiocephale," Colin continued. "See the bone-headed beasts butt their way to dominance. Meet the Dubreuillosaurus. See them gnaw the guts of a gasless Gasosaurus." And so on.

Next, Colin introduced Tracey to the dinosaurs above them, which inhabited the center of his island. "Meet the Quetzalcoatlus," he said. "Hear them chirp as they fly in circles overhead. Hear the first musical crib toy made for men." A slight laugh left Tracey's lips. Colin couldn't believe she liked his stupid joke, and without thinking, he kissed her on the cheek. Immediately, he wanted to apologize, but his mouth became a machine that he could no longer operate. Tracey fixed the machine when she pressed her lips to his, when he felt her tongue poke his throat. And once Colin regained control, he used his own tongue to push the pressure toward Tracey's mouth.

They kissed for a few minutes, until Tracey got up and walked toward the Latirhinuses. Colin had only kissed one other girl before this moment. Ecstatic, he continued his tour. "Meet the Triceratops," he said, pointing at the dinosaurs stretching from the left side of his bed to the back wall. "See the dinosaur equivalent to an elephant-hog with horns."

Tracey lay back down, holding the head of a Latirhinus in her hand.

"Meet the Deinonychus." Colin directed his finger down the center of his island. "See its claws cleave the feathers from a Velociraptor."

Colin thought that Tracey had stopped listening. Ever since she grabbed the duck-billed dinosaur, she'd been massaging his inner-thighs with it. He turned toward her and they swapped spit for a few more minutes. Then she put his touring hand under her shirt. And that's when he realized she hadn't been wearing a bra. He rubbed his palm over her breasts, gently pinching her nipples. Slowly, he started to lift Tracey's shirt, but his hand froze at her belly as he heard Marvin Gaye's "Let's Get It On" seep through the sheets. He realized that the music came from his brother's

26

movie, and he remembered that his island consisted of nothing more than a bed in a blanket fort. Tracey, though, didn't seem to mind their simulated solitude. She sat up and lifted her shirt over her head, and for the first time in Colin's life, he saw a topless woman without virtual assistance.

"Use this," Tracey said, handing Colin the rubber Latirhinus head.

Tracey lay back down and they resumed, sans one shirt. Colin pressed the paleoart against her, tracing the contours of her breasts with the duckbill. Then he kissed her neck, his tongue careening to caress her clavicle. Colin couldn't believe that this was actually happening. Tracey, the girl he'd been eyeing ever since he started school, the only human whose image he could conjure whenever he went to whack off the past fourteen days, now lay half-naked in his room, and his mouth moved to nurse her left nipple. The Latirhinus dangled over the side of the bed, so Tracey yanked it out of Colin's hand. And the moment his tongue tasted her tit, she pressed the duckbill against his cock, and he shot his seed into his shorts. Fuck, he thought, as a moan slipped through his lips.

"Did you just come?" Tracey asked, and Colin thought she looked amused.

Colin lifted his mouth from her nipple and unconvincingly denied the accusation. Despite his embarrassment, he couldn't bring himself to lift the Latirhinus from his crotch.

Colin continued his private tour by showing his guest the last corner of his collection. Tracey smiled at him, said she thought that he was so cute, before she began massaging the space beneath his balls with the hadrosaur's head. "Meet the mighty Tyrannosaurus Rex," Colin said. "See the only lizard deranged enough to tyrannize any dinosaur that wanders into its territory."

27

Into the Forest (Chapter Six)

COLIN WANTED NOTHING MORE than to stand still and lean against a tree as he tried to figure out a plan that would fix this situation, but it just wouldn't happen. Despite his many attempts to quit, he continued bouncing along to his two-step. And to make matters worse, the roar of a Tyrannosaurus Rex flooded the forest.

When he had first awakened, he could only think about his urge to urinate. He stood up and shimmied to the nearest tree, heedless of his surroundings. Even the nausea that coincides with suddenly standing didn't deter him on his path to pee.

Uncontrollably, his fluids flew through the air, splashing against his shins as he two-stepped before the tree, and once his bodily pain passed into pleasure, he finally observed the world around him. It took him a minute to realize that he should have been in an ice cave. It took him even longer to understand that his non-stop dancing before a breathing, rainbow-shaded forest meant that his journey on the *Jolly Dancer* had existed as more than just a communal dream. Knowing that dancing dinosaurs could be watching him, Colin quickly became self-conscious of his two-step.

He sluggishly shimmied back to their camp. When he arrived and his movements morphed back into a two-step, his upper body bouncing to the beat of his feet, he realized that Joe had vanished. This discovery didn't initially worry Colin. As he watched Emma sleep, he convinced himself that his brother had gotten up to pee, or that he had decided to survey the forest. And once he returned, Joe would show them the best path to take through the trees.

But after what Colin believed to be thirty minutes, although in the Days of the Dinosaur it could have been closer to thirty seconds, his two-step, in combination with Joe's lack of return, caused him to nibble his nails. Clouds crawled through Colin's mind. His thoughts swirled between the pact he'd made with Emma his second year at college and what had happened to Joe. He desired to stop dancing so he could meditate through the murk, but the constant motion heightened his anxiety. He invented thousands of hypothetical scenarios that, at their best, had Joe wandering the forest forever, and at their worst, had him already deteriorating inside the belly of a dancing dinosaur.

Colin distracted himself by letting a thick glob of spit leave his lips for the ground, where seconds later, when the Tyrannosaurus Rex flooded the forest with his roar, he watched it scatter into hundreds of tiny globules. Colin wondered if his saliva could feel fear. He looked up and realized that Emma had awoke. She used her hands to shake the sleep from her eyes, and she looked worried. She asked Colin if he had seen Joe.

Colin shook his head and realized that he, and not his saliva, feared the roar. And he understood he hadn't reserved his fear solely for himself. Most of it he lent to Joe, who, according to Colin's intuition, resided in the Tyrannosaurus Rex's possession.

"Colin, we fucked up," she said. "We've failed." The forest fell a few shades darker, as if the color were being vacuumed out of the Earth.

"We haven't failed," he said, two-stepping next to Emma, who still lay on the forest floor. "Joe's alive. I feel it."

"But I forgot to bring his antibiotics," Emma cried.

Colin flinched, but before he could respond, before Emma even got to her feet, the shrubs rustled. Besides his wilting two-step, his body froze. A slight breeze of thyme bred with basil slowly seeped from the bushes, which sported leaves shaped like yellow lily pads. As the dinosaur started to materialize, the forest regained its color. Colin remained calcified.

Piece by piece it appeared, as if the bushes were birthing it.

The tail slithered into view first, but before Colin could blame the rustling on a snake, a pair of paws emerged. A body followed its feet, and then the head arose. The dinosaur came into view as if it had been lying on its back in the bushes, setting down its hind legs first before flipping the rest of its body onto its feet. And only once Colin and the dinosaur danced face to face did he allow himself to believe that this animal truly was an Apatosaurus. He sighed with relief.

"Hello," the dinosaur said, awkwardly two-stepping with four feet. "I'm Rose."

"Rose," Colin said, more to himself than to the dinosaur. "Colin," he said, pointing at himself and grinning stupidly, scarcely able to fathom that he knew an Apatosaurus by name.

The longer he looked at the dinosaur, the less sure he became of her color scheme. She certainly consisted of the same green, purple, and blue tie-dye skin as the dinosaurs the day before, but all three shades seemed to be in constant motion, moving along the Apatosaurus's flesh as if each color itself were alive.

Once Colin had thoroughly studied the dinosaur's strange skin, he realized he had danced with Rose the previous night. The feelings of love that had flourished during their psychedelic swing returned immediately, and their intensity grew with immense speed. But before he could do anything embarrassing, Emma interrupted him.

"Where's Joe?" she said, frantically.

For every ounce of love the Apatosaurus's appearance sparked within Colin, it seemed to create an equally strong sense of panic in Emma. He wondered if his desire for the dinosaur were obvious, and if it were, would it trigger Emma's trauma? His friend's perfect two-step began to falter, and because he had never seen her make a mistake while dancing, her rhythmless twitch sobered his infatuation with Rose just enough to allow his brain to function.

"Rose," Colin said, trying to find an expression that would balance his glee and gloom. And although his smile favored the former, his voice contained the latter. "Have you seen my brother? He's been missing all morning."

"Yes," Rose said, glancing nervously at the forest behind her, "but we need to start moving. It's dangerous out in the open like this. When we're safe, I'll tell you what happened."

"We need to know now," Emma said.

"It's too dangerous."

"I think we should listen to her, Emma," Colin said, taking a step toward Rose. She slid her tail into his hand. Pleasure permeated his face.

"Christ, Colin," Emma said. "Whose side are you on?"

"Nobody's," Colin said, dropping the dinosaur's tail. Emma and Rose both shot him a glance. "I mean," he continued, "I just want to save Joe. And right now, I think Rose is our best option." She slithered her tail into his hand again.

"Stop thinking with your goddamn dick," Emma said.

"I'm not," Colin said, his face flushed with sweat. Turning his focus to Rose, he said, "You'll show us how to get him back the second we're safe?"

"The second we're safe," Rose agreed. She glanced backward again, and added, "I'll tell you everything as soon as I can."

"But," Emma said, and her voice caught a couple of times before the words came, "I need to know if he's alive."

Colin didn't know if he wanted to hear the answer to the question, but before he could decide, he heard Rose saying, "He's absolutely alive, and they'll be treating him like a king for the next three days, fattening him up for the champion's feast. We'll have plenty of time to save him once we're safe, but we're no help to your friend if they find us first."

"Three days!" Emma exclaimed, bordering hysteria. "He might need his antibiotics now. Where is he?" She started stomping her feet against the ground, galloping toward Rose as tears rolled down her cheeks.

"Relax," Rose said, stretching her neck, using her head to keep Emma out of fighting distance. "The Tyrannosaurus Task Force probably has him halfway to the House of Rex by now."

The moment Rose stopped speaking, she turned and boogalooed toward the bushes. She shifted her weight from foot to foot, bending her knees in the process, creating the illusion that she floated across the grassy floor. And as her tail disappeared into the forest, The Chambers Brothers' "Are You Ready" clamored from the trees.

Emma looked at Colin and said, "The Tyrannosaurus Task Force?"

Colin shrugged. He wondered if Emma's eyes were actually as

31

wide as fists or if he had just imagined it. Regardless, he began to boogaloo into the forest after Rose, only he couldn't recreate the floating effect.

"Colin!" Emma said. "Where do you think you're going? We need to find Joe."

Colin glanced over his shoulder and said, "That's what I'm doing. Without Rose's help, we will never find him."

"How do you know she isn't lying?"

"I don't," Colin said. He saw Emma stubbornly stomp her feet as she started to follow him. But then Colin's stiff knees boogalooed him into a dense layer of bushes and trees, and he closed his eyes as he forced his face through the branches and leaves.

Once he danced past the initial line of foliage, the pressure of the plants faded. Carefully, Colin opened his eyes, and he saw both the bushes and the trees clear a path before him, as if they were boogalooing along the forest floor. About a hundred feet ahead, the path narrowed to a wall of multicolored plants, but no matter how far his dance carried him, the distance of the clearing never decreased.

Despite the consistency of the clearing, Colin's vision never ceased manipulating what he perceived. At first the space seemed to shrink. His vision zoomed in on the plant wall until the clearing appeared to span just a few feet. Colin saw every leaf and twig vividly, and as the slightest scent of amber incense seeped from the plants, he even believed he could see the tip of Rose's tail. He closed his eyes and prepared for the pressure of the branches and leaves to resume. But after dancing a distance that must have closed the gap, he opened his lids and discovered that he'd never make it to the end of the ever-expanding tunnel, which seemed to stretch for thousands of yards. The clearing became a blurry, hazy space where all the leaves and branches danced in the breeze. Although Colin felt relieved that he wouldn't have to fight his way through another dense segment of forest, he started feeling anxious, too, because he believed he would never reach a destination in these woods regardless of the distance he danced. His anxiety spiked when he could no longer distinguish one hair on the back of his hand from another. The hairs became interwoven vines, growing until they merged with the shrubs and the trees around him, and Colin and the forest became a cohesive being. And just as he thought he couldn't handle being glued to the ground with the vegetation any longer, the blurry haze lifted and the breeze stopped. Colin broke the connection between the vines and his body with his boogaloo, causing the plants to rearrange themselves until the rainbow wall stood only a few feet away, and he could see the tip of Rose's tail once more.

The second time Colin experienced this cycle his anxiety had decreased significantly. He felt pretty confident that when he closed in on the plant wall, he would not actually make it, and when he became one with the forest, it would not be permanent. During the third cycle, his anxiety had practically vanished. And as he experienced the fourth, he enjoyed the visuals and synced what he saw, as well as his boogaloo, with the soulful sounds of The Chambers Brothers.

With each new cycle, "Are You Ready" played all the way through, and just before the fifth round began, Colin realized Emma boogalooed beside him. He tried asking her what had happened, if she had found it spooky at first, too, and if so, he'd ask if she were enjoying it yet. But when he opened his mouth, the song's volume exploded in his ears. If he'd actually spoken aloud, he couldn't hear his own voice. Colin tried to communicate with Emma several times over the next hour before he could accept that it would not work.

Cycles came and went and Colin stayed content as he danced further into the forest. But eventually, the repetition of "Are You Ready" caused Colin to bite his nails again.

Emma's presence started becoming less apparent. As Colin danced through the clearing, he felt forsaken, and his future yielded increasingly less hope. Though he held onto the last scraps for what felt like weeks, he ultimately understood that he was destined to dance in these continuously cyclical spatial shifts forever.

And then the cycle finally ceased.

—

Colin danced. Despite his many attempts to quit, he continued bouncing along to his boogaloo. Emma grooved beside him and Rose danced up ahead. Trees reached down from the grass sky and somewhere below his feet, deep within the translucent Earth, he saw the underside of the sun. Colin became so confused by the geographical change that he couldn't contain any other thought or feeling, as if he were pressed into mental paralysis.

"We're here," Rose shouted, twisting her neck toward Emma and Colin.

The dinosaur's voice brought Colin out of his paralysis. After processing her words, he said, "Here?"

"Home," Rose said, happily. "The Astral of the Apatosaurus."

"Great," Emma said. "Now what's the Astral of the Apatosaurus?"

"It's a celestial sphere embodied by a tree between the Astral Plane and the Days of the Dinosaur," Rose said. "While we inhabit the Astral of the Apatosaurus, no Earthly being can endanger us."

As Rose said this, Colin finally caught up to her. He continued his boogaloo between Emma and the Apatosaurus, and as he looked at the landscape, he discovered they were dancing toward a clearing. A green prairie stretched in the sky before him, and in its center stood a massive tie-dye tree. As they approached the Astral of the Apatosaurus, Colin saw a series of tree houses carved out of its spine, and it reminded him of a wooden flute hanging from the hands of a grassy god.

Astral of the Apatosaurus (Chapter Seven)

THE LONGER COLIN LOOKED at Rose's home, the more he began to understand what he saw. The planet from which the Astral of the Apatosaurus grew essentially appeared the same as the prehistoric Earth he had recently been inhabiting, only inverted. The ground became the relative equivalent to what had been the clouds, and the crystallized grass sky had previously been the forest floor. The same trees grew from the grass, only now they reached down toward the translucent ground beneath his feet. And below the tree in the center of the clearing, Colin saw a circle of Apatosauruses concoct a conga-line, their heads disappearing into the hollowed-out house above them as they danced.

"Are we safe yet?" Emma asked.

"Yes," Rose said, "but—"

"What's happened to Joe?"

Colin continued to butcher his boogaloo as his blood rushed to his brain, as if he were holding an endless handstand. As he danced closer to Rose's home, gravity pulled him toward the grass sky, but it couldn't lift him off the translucent ground. His thoughts throbbed, and he wondered if his feet were nailed to the underside of a cloud. The Apatosauruses before him sashayed from side to side, casually advancing their conga-line, and he stretched his neck toward the apparent comfort of the tree house, hoping to alleviate some of the agonizing pressure.

Beside him, Rose cleared her throat as well as a dancing dinosaur could. She took a deep breath and slowly began to speak. "I can only say what I saw." Her voice sounded suppressed and high pitched, as if they were buried underwater. "As to what it means, you'll have to wait for an official statement from the Conga-Line Caucus."

Colin danced faster. Not only did the Conga-Line Caucus present potential relief to his hammering head pain, they also knew how to rescue Joe. But as he cruised closer, their conga-line turned considerably chaotic, and every time they completed a rotation, their dance increasingly resembled Jell-O. Their rubbery convulsions reminded Colin of childhood, of his dad shaking one of his pristine colored pencils between his fingers as he raised his head from his craft.

"Why're they jiggling?" Colin asked.

"The gravity's getting to them," Rose said.

"What do you mean?"

"The Astral of the Apatosaurus was created in haste to protect us from the Tyrannosaurus Task Force. During its construction, its creators didn't bother inverting gravity like the rest of our Astral. Inverting gravity is a much longer process than landscape, and the tree was only supposed to be temporary."

The Caucus continued to digress until the dance dissolved to a rubbery conga-line orgy. As the dinosaurs advanced in their circle, their bodies merged together, creating an Apatosaurus tornado. The gravitational pull increased, and Colin felt his spirit split from his flesh again and again as it attempted to ascend to the grass sky.

"What else can you tell us about Joe?" Emma asked. "What did you see?"

Emma's voice eased the pressure slightly, which had started pounding high-fives into Colin's eardrums. He faced Rose as she prepared to divulge the details of his twin brother and best friend's abduction, and he lifted his right hand to shield the Conga-Line Caucus from his peripheral vision. He wrestled with the dynamite dancing in his skull.

"I first heard your friend seconds before I started my journey home," Rose said, slowing down her dance. "He spoke loudly, probably sleep-dancing just inside the forest. And shortly after that, I heard the song of the Tyrannosaurus Task Force." She boogalooed in place, and Colin and Emma paused their progress. "I shimmied my way back to the forest's edge as fast as I could. But by the time I arrived, your friend was gone. I bunny-hopped back into the forest and headbanged through the trees, but when I found him, he had already been captured by the Tyrannosaurus Task Force. Mercilessly, they led him through the forest with a melancholy Macarena." Rose stood there in silence for a few moments, casting shadows over Colin and Emma as she shook her head from side to side. She said, "I'm so sorry."

Colin wondered if Apatosauruses had the capacity to cry. Rose certainly looked like she wanted to, but he couldn't detect any tears rolling down her neck.

"It's okay," Colin said. "We'll get him back." He reached out and grabbed her tail, and to his relief, she smiled. He smiled, too, and in his mind he winged his arms and flapped, kicking his feet as if they were shoveling dirt. Once he finished his celebratory funky chicken, he realized he had become aroused. Horrified at his lack of bodily control, Colin tried to hide his love from the longneck, which caused his awkwardly stiff boogaloo to become even more corpse-like.

"It's not okay," Emma hissed, and Colin silently thanked her for the distraction. She continued, "Why didn't you wake us the moment they took Joe?"

"I panicked," Rose said. "I've never seen the Tyrannosaurus Task Force take somebody before." She paused momentarily, and Colin thought he saw her eyes roll till her sockets were bright white. "I'm sorry," she said again, as if they were the only words her eyes could see in her soul. Any happiness Colin had instilled when he took her tail had evaporated entirely.

"That's not good enough," Emma said. "We could have been a few hours closer to saving him if you had woken us immediately."

"There's nothing any of us can do about it now," Colin said, hoping to help lift Rose's spirits. "The only way we can save Joe is by working together. Arguing over whose fault it is won't solve anything."

"Okay sure," Emma said. "But what do we do now?" Her voice cracked. "How do we get him back?"

"I'll take you to the Conga-Line Caucus." Rose immediately began clogging toward the circle of Apatosauruses. Glancing back, she added, "They'll help."

Eagerly, Emma clogged after Rose, and behind her, Colin clogged up the rear.

———

As Colin's clog brought him near the Conga-Line Caucus, he could hear The Champ's "Tequila" booming from the hollowed out tree house. Each time the dinosaurs stopped to shout "tequila," they uncoordinatedly kicked a front and back paw, and lowered their heads from the house so they could sing their song to the inverted Earth. Immediately afterward, they returned their heads to the tree, shaking their bodies forward as their circular conga-line advanced.

When Rose finally clogged her way to the Apatosauruses, she bit one of their tails and pulled, which caused the dinosaur to conga in place. The next Apatosaurus in line quickly crashed into it, temporarily turning its body to rubber before its conga became stationary, too. This process repeated itself until every Apatosaurus in line danced in place, and only then did they all lower their heads to investigate what had brought their dance to a halt.

"Who dares interrupt the Conga-Line Caucus?" one of the Apatosauruses asked, and together all the dinosaurs dashed their heads from side to side, searching for the culprit.

Colin tried to stop clogging. The combination of the Apatosaurus's cruel, cold voice and gravity's constantly increasing push toward the grass sky killed any lingering motive to dance. He meditated on being still, on his body sailing up into the tree, but he only clogged more relentlessly, and his body's blood continued to cannonball into his brain.

"It was me!" Rose said, giggling at the elderly Apatosauruses.

How could she laugh under this atmospheric pressure? How could the Apatosauruses keep their conga-line from creeping back to chaos? Colin envied the dinosaurs and their apparent calm as he wrestled to keep his own clog under relative control.

"Who is this me?" asked the same Apatosaurus in a slightly more ridiculous tone, as if it were trying to stifle laughter.

The dinosaur's voice sounded impossibly high-pitched, like a pissed-off Smee. Colin couldn't tell if he and Emma were in danger. Apatosauruses were vegetarians, so the dinosaurs wouldn't eat them, but these animals were almost twice the size of Rose, who, stretching at least sixty feet, should have been nearly full-grown. These mega-Apatosauruses were so big they could easily crush Colin and Emma without making them their meal.

"Reggie," Rose said, "stop playing around. This is serious."

Colin let the air out of his chest. Rose continued, "These are my friends." She pointed to Colin and Emma with her tail. Colin brushed his long brown hair out of his eyes and Emma smirked as they clogged. "And the Tyrannosaurus Task Force has taken their friend. They need me to guide them through the forest to the House of Rex. Please, may I go?"

"You actually want to go? Have you even seen them dance?"

"Yes," Rose said, pleading. "I danced with them last night. I danced with Colin," she tilted her head toward him and smiled, "and Emma danced with their missing friend, Joe. Trust me, Reggie, they're fantastic dancers."

Colin stuck his fingers into his ears to dig out the wax. His fingers came back clean. Did Rose actually believe he could dance?

"Of course I trust you," Reggie said. "But the dangers this journey will pose, to not just yourself but the entire clan, are unimaginable. We need to make sure they are the ones. They need to beat our best before we equip them with a guide."

"They will," Rose said.

Reggie leaned his head against the ground and grimaced, and Rose used her tail to scoop Colin and Emma onto her back before clogging aboard. Colin silently apologized to the mega-Apatosaurus for making him bend down against gravity and for the pain their additional weight presented. But as the dinosaur lifted them toward the treetop, his face relaxed, and Colin felt relieved. He quietly said to Rose, "We will what?"

Turning to Colin and Emma, Rose said, "In order for the Apatosauruses to allow me to guide you on your quest, you must first prove to them that you're worthy of our help. You must beat them in a dance-off."

"Crap," Colin said, and seconds later, Reggie rested his head on a platform inside the hollowed-out tree house where he had previously held the Conga-Line Caucus. Rose used her tail to lift

Colin and Emma off her back, and they followed her onto the platform.

Slowly, the platform started to morph back into the wooden pathway from which it extended. Being inside the tree house decreased the gravitational pull a bit, and Colin's head started to clear. The circular path they danced on spanned along the interior of the tree house. It remained roughly twenty feet wide. At opposite ends, the path parted from its ring, stretching along the branches outside the hollowed-out house. And once the platform had completely succumbed to the path, the walkway began to sway as if the tree's bark were breathing.

"It's okay," Emma said, "Joe and I are at the top of our dance class. As long as you let me guide you, we will win."

"Okay," Colin said, and as he continued to clog, he discovered that the tree house walls were covered in cave paintings. The artwork conveyed meaning through motion, as if it were a film the Apatosauruses had etched into the wood. The images depicted coupled dinosaurs doing a strange dance. After their performance, the cave paintings described the rebuttal of humans, all of whom danced slightly better than Colin. The people in the paintings crossed their wrists and jerked them up and down like they were galloping on a horse. They hopped from foot to foot. Without fail, at the end of each dance-off, the Apatosauruses were crowned the champions. Despite Emma's ability to dance, Colin remained unconvinced he'd be able to save his brother. "Can't Rose take my place?"

Emma looked to Rose hopefully, but she shook her head. "Colin," Emma said, "you can do this. Just follow my lead, and most importantly, don't fuck this up. I swear to god, if you're the reason we can't save Joe, you won't have to worry about taking the trip without a guide. I'll fucking kill you myself."

Rose wrapped her tail around Colin and squeezed. He wished he could lose himself in this embrace forever, or at least long enough to know that this meant love. But the hug came to completion within seconds, and the moment Rose let go, he knew he had to prepare himself for the dance-off.

"Rose," Reggie commanded, "take them to the dance floor."

Rose slid her tail between Colin's hands, and Emma placed hers on his shoulders. In a conga-line of their own, Rose led her friends out of the tree house and onto the wooden path, which quickly widened to at least fifty feet, and took them up into the depths of the tree.

As Colin stepped out of the house, The Doors' "Strange Days" immediately rained down on him from the crystallized grass above. Gravitational relief rested just before him, but no matter how quickly he chased it, he couldn't catch it. The relief taunted him, causing him to regain the head pressure he had released while inside the tree house. As the increasing pain mixed with Ray Manzarek's darkly melodic Moog, Colin felt his body fast-forward. And with Rose guiding their conga-line, Colin zoomed past Apatosauruses until he came to another hollowed out tree house.

Once they entered this house, the song suddenly ceased and the speed at which Colin's body functioned returned to normal. The path shrank back to being twenty feet wide, and the gravitational force started to recede. As they danced through the house, Colin noticed that different vegetables lined the interior walls. His stomach croaked, but before he could snatch a plant to eat, never mind study the variety of vegetables that composed the diets of these dinosaurs, the conga-line had led him out of the food house. "Strange Days" and his body's increased speed resumed simultaneously as the path widened once more, and the grandeur of the crystallized grass sky's kaleidoscopic rays stained his skin an emerald green.

Inhabiting higher altitude caused the atmospheric pressure to simmer, allowing Colin's mind to match the speed at which his dancing body traversed the tree's landscape. As he congaed up the path, he observed its complete architecture concurrently. The path he danced along zigzagged up the tree, its foundations built on the branches. When he reached the end of one branch, its tip touched another, which would take his conga-line back to the tree's body, a little closer to its roots. Each time the path took him through the body of the tree, it shrank back to twenty feet and circled the interior wall of a hollowed-out house. Rose would then lead the conga-line halfway around the circle and out the other side. This pattern repeated itself five times on each side of the tree, creating houses on ten separate levels. The dinosaurs had hollowed out the entire tree except for each house's ceiling.

The lowest point of the path ended to the right of the tree house that contained the cave paintings. Had Rose taken the conga-line in that direction, Colin realized the path would have taken them to a massive wooden elevator. He watched the elevator directly below him as he started to dance his way back to the tree's spine. The wooden platform descended toward the translucent ground, and once it landed, Reggie and the other elderly Apatosauruses belly-danced aboard. The elevator then began to ascend the tree, and just before Colin entered the third house, he realized that given the zigzag nature of the path, the elevator stopped at every other floor starting with the first.

Colin again felt the strange sensation of his body slowing down to its regular rhythm. Although he had finally seen the Astral of the Apatosaurus in its entirety, the lingering headache kept him from fully wrapping his mind around the tree. And being inside the hygiene house hardly helped. Along one half of the path Colin saw a series of sinks with toothbrushes protruding from the wall above them, and down the other half showerheads lined the wall a few feet above the walkway. Colin wondered why these Apatosauruses needed to brush their teeth and shower, but before he came to any conclusions, he danced out the door and under the sounds of "Strange Days" once more. The path widened as he watched the mega-Apatosauruses rise past him in the elevator on the other side of the tree.

The tree houses kept coming and going, and after he passed through the sixth house—the first of four sleeping quarters—Colin forced himself to forget the scenery and focus on the imminent dance-off.

He envisioned himself in Emma's hands, his body being directed this way and that as he moved to the music. In his mind, he practiced letting go, loosening his limbs so Emma could bend them according to her every whim. Satisfied with his ability to let go, Colin squeezed Rose's tail as he congaed up the path through the tree houses.

When they reached the tree house on the tenth floor, which had been constructed approximately thirty-five feet below the crystallized grass sky, the gravitational pressure evaporated entirely. As the pain faded, Colin felt anything could happen, especially winning a dance-off. If Rose thought he had danced fantastically before, she would soon think he grooved phe-fucking-nomenally. And through the process of blowing Rose's mind, he and Emma would undertake their quest to save his brother. Nothing could possibly keep them from rescuing Joe.

As they passed through the house, which, unlike the other houses, had solid wood flooring throughout, Colin observed the room from where the audience would watch him dance. The walls surrounding this portion of the tree were comprised of panes of glass instead of breathing bark. And depending on which panel the Apatosauruses looked through, they could see the dance-floor from a variety of angles ranging anywhere from a close-up to a long shot.

Rose led the conga-line through the audience house as quickly as possible. Thirty seconds later, they danced out of the house and onto a swaying bridge.

The bridge took Colin and the conga-line to the dance-floor: A neon purple mushroom that sprouted from the grass sky near the Astral of the Apatosaurus. As Colin stepped onto the squishy gills of the mushroom's underside, the world became black. And a minute later, neon purple spores rained up from the mushroom's bottom, and the crystallized grass sky glowed emerald green.

"Try not to think about what you're doing out there." Emma stared into Colin's eyes.

He wondered if her pupils were really growing past her irises. Like a pencil poking through paper, he thought.

"Just relax and follow my lead," Emma said, her pupils retreating back beneath their lids, "and please, for the love of dance, don't do anything stupid."

"Don't worry," Colin said, "I got this. Let's save Joe!"

Colin looked across the dance-floor. On the other side, he saw a group of the green, purple, and blue tie-dye dancing dinosaurs that he had come to associate with Apatosauruses. They stretched in a circle, bobbling their heads from side to side, their bodies partially covered in neon war paint.

Dormitory (Chapter Eight)

COLIN AND JOE DROVE Colin's pterodactyl-themed VW Bus up to Seattle from San Francisco. When they arrived at their university, students volunteering on move-in day directed them to their dormitory. They parked the VW Bus in the dorm's underground parking garage and went up to find their room. They were directed to the East wing of the third floor and given their room keys. They picked their beds and headed back to the car to bring up their luggage.

When they entered the parking garage beneath the dormitory, Colin saw some girls gawking at his pterodactyl-themed VW Bus. He immediately blushed and his brother flipped them off. In all, it took eight trips to unload everything they brought, most of which consisted of Colin's paleoart museum. But once they finally moved everything into their new home, they cracked open some beers they brought with them from San Francisco and began to slowly settle into their room.

Before Colin setup his dinosaur art museum, he and his brother made their respective beds and emptied the suitcases containing their clothes. Joe finished unpacking his suitcase by setting up his record player on his desk. Colin finished by removing a blue and green Apatosaurus wall tapestry from his suitcase. He held it close to his chest. He lowered his head to peck it. Colin slowly unwrapped the tapestry, revealing a framed photograph of Victoria Warby, the original ballet break-dancer, leading him in an unprofessionally playful polka. He had just turned five at the time. This photo contained the last memory he had of her, and he hugged it once more.

"Where should we put mom?" Colin asked Joe.

"It was your last dance, man," Joe said, "the last thing you two shared the night she died. Put it wherever it comforts you the most."

"Thanks," Colin said, setting the photograph on his nightstand.

"Of course," Joe said, and he stood up and moved toward the record player on his desk. "Check this out," he said, and as Sly and the Family Stone's "Dance to the Medley" roared, he strolled to the center of the room. "I've been practicing some of mom's moves in my spare time. I've kept it secret because I hoped a surprise might make this transition away from all the dinosaur shit you had to leave at home a little less of a bummer." He bent over and pressed his forehead against the ground, and using his feet as propellers, pushed himself into a handless headspin.

Colin sat up. He hadn't seen someone do a truly handless headspin since his mother had done it for him and Joe in their bedroom when they failed to find sleep as children. Of course, he'd seen plenty of handless headspins since, but those were initially propelled by the dancers' hands before they went handless. With the exception of his mother, he had never actually seen a dancer do a truly handless headspin.

A minute into his spin, once he had found that familiar, faultless groove, Joe incorporated ballet into his breakdance. He held one leg straight, toes pointing toward the sky, while he extended his other leg behind his body, forming an upright L from the waist down. He bent the horizontal leg, pressing his foot just above the side of the straight leg's kneecap. After holding the handless headspin pirouette for a couple of minutes, Joe pushed his legs together, stretching them as far as he could. He began to run in place, his legs galloping through the air. After a few successive sprints, he air leapt his legs into the splits. He held his *grand jeté* for a few seconds before bracing his legs for an aerial landing. Joe continued combining *grands jetés* with his handless headspin for several more minutes, but when the song faded, he tipped over and fell to his feet.

Colin stared at his brother, who stood in the center of the room with a nervous smile. Colin forgot how to speak.

After a minute, Joe said, "I've been working on that ever since I saw mom do it for us as kids. What do you think?"

"It's perfect," Colin said.

"Thanks man! But I know I fucked up those pirouettes. So honestly, how close was it to mom's?"

"Perfect," Colin said, the only word he could muster. He didn't think anyone could match their mother's ability to dance. Sure, his dad had kept them away from the scene ever since their mother died in her dancing accident—she performed a new ballet break-dance when she broke too hard, her body splitting at the waist on stage—but even then, if there were a new Victoria Warby out there, it'd make headlines. And yet, Joe, the new Victoria Warby, had been mastering their mother's move in secret under their father's roof all these years. Watching his brother dance, Colin almost believed their mom had somehow resurrected herself. For the first time since she died, he believed that someone could be just as good, if not better, at ballet break-dancing as she. For the first time in his life, Colin believed he could relate to his mom. She was no longer an impossibly super-human dancer, but simply a super human. If his brother could ballet break-dance like her, why couldn't he? He just had to dance.

Joe didn't seem to believe Colin's praise. But that didn't matter. And because he didn't know what else to say, Colin asked, "Want to help me set up my museum?"

"I'd love to," Joe said, smiling.

Colin walked over to the biggest box. He pulled out the longneck Apatosaurus heads and slowly stroked them.

"Those look so real," Joe said, winking. "I just love me some dinosaurs!"

Joe didn't know shit about dinosaurs and never cared to learn. He couldn't even name the species he looked at, couldn't even comprehend that they were sauropods, his brother's absolute favorite. Colin believed his brother's lack of interest stemmed from a desire to spite their dad over banning them from dance. Moreover, his sculptures looked nothing like real Apatosauruses. For starters, they were certainly not actual size. Besides that, as far as their skin is concerned, it is scientifically possible that

Apatosauruses were partially covered in feathers just like Tyrannosaurus Rexes, as opposed to the fake scales scattered over the surface of his collected art. Nevertheless, he played along and said, "Thanks."

"Can I touch one?"

"Sure," Colin said, rolling his eyes, "you can touch all of them. But first, help me hang these sheets from the ceiling. We need to make some gallery space. And once we have that, we will create the most incredible paleoart exhibit anyone has ever seen."

THE APATOSAURUS QUADRILLE (CHAPTER NINE)

THE STEM OF THE MUSHROOM vibrated violently under the grass sky's emerald glow. The mushroom's cap wrinkled in waves. Colin began to feel seasick as the gills continued to rock back and forth, back and forth, and he wondered if this were what it would be like to be caught on the *Jolly Dancer* in the middle of a meteor shower. Every few seconds, the stem sent another shock through the mushroom.

After the first wave went over the edge of the cap, The Modern Lovers' "Astral Plane" reverberated from the mushroom's neon purple skin. Because of the waves, Colin's view of the Apatosauruses obscured in loops, and he saw the dinosaurs dance in choppy stop-motion. They formed two lines around the stalk. Both lines faced the other, and a sea of sixteen feet separated them. Once the song's instruments gained speed, the Apatosauruses advanced. As they met in the middle, they quickly twisted their tails before continuing to the other side.

When they met on their second advance, they used their heads simultaneously to smack their partner's bodies—clap, clap—in the same style as the fighting giraffes Colin had seen on television. Then, the Apatosauruses swapped partners and withdrew in the same fashion.

When the Apatosauruses were back in their lines, they advanced once more. When they reached their second partner, they didn't use their heads as whips. Instead, the Apatosauruses nearest the stem of the mushroom curled their necks until they spiraled like snakes, their heads resting against the gills of the fungi. Their necks began to bounce like springs.

The pulsation of the stem and the cap's resulting waves hadn't yet hindered Colin's perception of the Apatosaurus Quadrille. While his vision had been stunted each time a wave spread throughout the mushroom's cap, the dance had been easy to follow. But when the dinosaurs rolled back into view, Colin's eyes expanded as he watched the Apatosauruses somersaulting through the air. They were being sprung by their partners. They bounced from spring to spring to spring.

After the Apatosauruses had passed their partners the length of the circle, they uncoiled their necks, swapped partners, and retreated until the distance between the two lines shrank back to sixteen feet again. They had finished the first figure. And as it progressed into the second, Colin reached for Rose's tail, but she had vanished.

Colin hesitated, casting a quizzical look at the gills where Rose once stood, before turning to face the bridge. The air orbiting the bridge became kaleidoscopic, as if it were embodying hyperspace. And the bridge itself started to stretch, reminding Colin of a clown pulling an infinite amount of cloth from its mouth. But regardless of how far it expanded, Colin could never erase what he saw on the other side. In the audience house, Rose twisted her tail with another Apatosaurus.

And a black abyss blanketed his world.

From a distance, Colin could still hear faint echoes of "Astral Plane" as it bellowed throughout the blackness. But besides the song, nothing from the outside world penetrated this darkness. Colin could taste it on his tongue, feel it slide down his throat until the black permeated his lungs. And as he drowned in the darkness, he could only think about his psychedelic swing with Rose. He wanted to lace his limbs with her for the rest of his life. But she didn't love him. She loved someone of her own species. And the darkness pervaded.

When the song ceased echoing, a shimmering hand reached into the black and hauled Colin back to the dance-floor. The neon purple mushroom and the glowing emerald grass blinded him. The hand dragged him through the waves toward the stem.

49

Given her tone, Colin believed Emma had been reminding him of what he should and should not to do, as well as reiterating her threats should he fail. However, he lacked confidence about what she had actually said. *Hell* or *swell*, he wondered, and the rest of the sentence had already slipped away. Colin wanted to scream *I don't got this*, but the words kept on tumbling back down his throat. Without Rose's complete support, Colin did not want to dance.

He dared not look at the audience house again for fear of spotting Rose twisting her tail with that other Apatosaurus, which he knew would bring him a mental breakdown on the dance-floor. And once Emma had led him to the mushroom's pulsating stem, The Moody Blues' "Nights in White Satin" seeped from its spores. Colin closed his eyes and tried to let his limbs go limp in Emma's arms as he allowed the music to bathe him in heartbreak. But no matter how hard he tried, he couldn't control his body. He flailed.

"What the fuck is this?" Emma hissed. "Stop jerking around and let me lead you."

Colin couldn't stop. His limbs kept flailing as Emma swung him around the dance-floor. Despite his protests, she continued to lead his contorting body in their tattered tango, cursing him every step of the dance.

Eventually, Colin wore Emma out. She turned taciturn. Her seething seemed to match Colin's sadness, and as a result, they tried to out-flail each other. As Emma led him across the rolling dance-floor, their flaring limbs fought, making their movements shoot in every direction like schizophrenic firecrackers.

Near the end of the song, Colin finally began to loosen up. Emma jerked his limbs around for a few more seconds before she seemed to realize he had stopped resisting. By this point though, she looked furious, and she somehow found the strength to lift him over her head.

"Let me down," he said, terrified, "what do you think you're doing?" but she refused to listen. "How will this solve anything?"

Pointing her partner toward the sky, she led him away from the stem. As she carried Colin to the edge of the mushroom, he started to sweat. "Goddamnit, Emma, unhand me already. We will never win like this." He returned to flailing, and she threw

50

him past the gills toward the translucent ground. He closed his eyes and cursed her. He yelped.

Colin had travelled almost halfway across the cap before he opened his eyes and realized he was sliding, not falling. He felt like a drop of rain sailing over the surface of an umbrella. As he passed the middle of the mushroom, he started to ascend back up the other side toward the edge of the cap. He felt unending relief as he watched the underside of the moon shine deep below the surface of the translucent Earth.

As Colin slid closer to the lip of the mushroom, he saw the Apatosauruses watching him from the audience house. They leaned to their left, the same direction in which Colin slid. They used each other's bodies to keep themselves from falling, and they pushed the air with their tails as if they were aiding his progression. Their expressions shifted between hope and fear before their entire beings began to melt into a single soupy face. And after a moment more, Colin could no longer resist looking for Rose. He scanned the crowd until he saw her, and when he did, her expression gave him a small spark of hope. Rose's tail no longer twirled with the other Apatosaurus's. It now shielded her eyes from witnessing Colin's deathly descent as she leaned further than any of the other dinosaurs.

Rose only dropped her tail once Colin had slid a few yards from the lip of the mushroom. Their eyes met, and she leaned further to her left until she unintentionally toppled to the ground. Laughter replaced his fears, and as Rose stood back up, he believed he saw a smile spread across her face that almost matched his own.

Colin flew over the edge of the cap. Sailing through the air, he accidentally did a double aerial cartwheel before his feet touched the mushroom's underside, and the sounds of The Moody Blues' "Nights in White Satin" ceased. Despite shaking from side to side, Colin stuck the landing, as if the gilled ground had absorbed his feet.

The dinosaurs in the audience house danced slowly in silence. Colin took this as a sign signifying his brother's death sentence. He glanced at Emma on the other side of the mushroom. She looked livid. And then the Apatosauruses across the bridge broke into astonished applause.

Bau the Brontosaurus (Chapter Ten)

ROSE DID SOME KIND OF DINOSAUR RAIN DANCE as she scurried across the bridge. And when she made it to the mushroom, which no longer rippled, Reggie led the rest of the animals across in their ritualistic dance. Once all the Apatosauruses had moved onto the mushroom, Rose led them in the formation of a circle around the stem.

The Crazy World of Arthur Brown's "Fire" boomed from the mushroom's body and the dinosaurs began dancing counterclockwise. Colin and Emma pressed their backs against the skin of the stalk. The Apatosauruses began to chant. Colin heard them invoke the name of Bau again and again.

"What the hell is going on?" Emma whispered to Colin, who couldn't tell whether or not she shook because of her dancing or out of fear.

Colin looked at her and shrugged. Then he turned his attention back to the Apatosauruses.

They were beating their heads against their own bodies, enhancing the song's drum as they continued their chants. After a few minutes, their rain dance tapered off to a soundless boogie. It took another minute for Colin to realize that he and Emma now mirrored the moves of the Apatosauruses. And then the dinosaurs addressed them.

"Where'd you learn to dance like that?" Rose asked. "I've

never seen anything so strange." She beamed, and Colin returned the smile.

"That was nothing," Colin said. Despite the audience's previous applause, he still couldn't process his new skills.

"It truly was spectacular," Reggie admitted, his tone hinting at hope. "A uniquely original performance. Congratulations on being crowned the new dance-off champions!"

"Really?" Emma asked. Her eyes narrowed.

Reggie curled his snout into an upside-down rainbow and nodded.

"Then lead us to Joe," Emma said, her words flattening the Apatosaurus's face.

Before Emma spoke, Colin hadn't been thinking about his brother. He still pondered the crown. He had hoped it would be a glistening gold, but now he started to think it would be more of a metaphorical award because nothing had been presented to him yet. And then Emma's words started to sink in, and he realized that their victory meant Rose would guide him on their journey. "Yeah," Colin said, "when can we leave?"

"Soon," Rose promised, "but first, you must hear the Prophecy of Bau before they gift me to you as your guide. And then they'll provide us with provisions as they send us off into the forest."

Colin nodded. As he thought about how far they had come and how far they still had to go, hunger stung his belly like a bee. Emma stayed silent, too, and Reggie prepared to present the prophecy.

"Before I begin," Reggie said, clearing his throat, "you must understand that we didn't always live like this." Colin struggled listening to Reggie's words. His mind had been crippled by visual puzzles. Slowly, they started to solve themselves as he watched the mushroom's gills swirl, and then leafy furniture began to grow. Neon green couches lifted the dinosaurs toward the grass sky, sweeping them up by their underbellies as their legs dangled over the sides. Then Emma followed suit. There were only a few Apatosauruses left dancing when Colin felt an armchair swoop him off his feet, scooping him into the air until his head rested against the grass sky.

"Many climates ago," he heard Reggie say as his puzzlement passed, "dinosaurs of every species coexisted comfortably. They had no leader. For every need they had, the land answered in abundance. They lived in a world where unnatural death plagued no dinosaur. They lived in a world where no animal, young or old, had to choose between going hungry or eating their friend. However, everything changed when their universe burped.

"It was a sunny summer day when the flaming Meteor of Mystical Movement shimmied through the sky, and after it crashed into the southwest corner of the island, a violent force followed, shaking the floor beneath the dinosaurs' feet. The story goes that the ground became alive, opening many different parts of its body, as if the Earth were formed by a militia of mouths. For the first time in our history, dinosaurs died to danger, cannibalized by the ground on which they stood. And although no animal could begin to guess the carnage that was to come, everyone understood that their world would never be the same." Reggie shook his head and sighed.

Colin gloomily glanced at Emma. She looked worried and he wondered who pondered a more gruesome fate for Joe. He wished his brother good vibes before shifting his focus to Rose. She took a bite out of the couch she lounged on, inspiring Colin to try a mouthful of his own chair. He took a big bite out of its right arm. It tasted surprisingly spicy, like jalapeño lettuce. He wanted more, but before he could take another bite, Reggie continued. "The first change our ancestors noticed was that whenever they stood, they could not stop shaking. They realized the meteor's dance that shook their land temporarily would never leave those who called it home. To this day the dance doesn't affect us when we sit or sleep, but no one understands why we receive these fleeting moments of peace.

"The true tragedy that accompanied the quaking Earth is not what fell into its mouth, but what came out. For the meteor was a seed, and from it sprouted a massive mushroom that the Tyrannosaurus Rex promptly marked as his territory." Reggie peered into Colin's eyes, and he felt the dinosaur's intensity sear his skin. He wanted to look away, but something about the Apatosaurus made him feel as if it would be wrong to do so. Reggie finally split the connection, spending a full minute staring at Emma. Colin relaxed and took a second bite out of his chair's arm. Could delicious leafy furniture scream? The dinosaur resumed his speech. "Hours after the meteor crashed and the quaking mushroom had been claimed, a loud shriek shook the bones of every dinosaur throughout the land. Shortly after that, our ancestors saw the transformed Tyrannosaurus Rex for the first time. He came with an army of genetically modified dinosaurs. Today, the descendants of his army are the only creatures to roam our Earth alongside the Tyrannosaurus Rex. As far as we know, the Astral of the Apatosaurus is the sole safe haven for the dinosaurs of old. For we have learned from our ancestors that when the Tyrannosaurus Rex brought his army to their paradise, they massacred many species, and the few they left alive, they enslaved.

"Our ancestors were cooped up in the Cesspool Cell deep below the surface of the House of Rex. In this dank dungeon, Apatosauruses were commanded to build dinosaur-themed pirate ships, and if our predecessors refused to work, they'd be whipped and starved, and eventually eaten. It was under these conditions that they escaped." Even though it looked like he tried to contain it, a proud smile spread across Reggie's colorful lips.

"Of course," he went on, "the escape would not have been possible if it weren't for the Astralsauruses. After our ancestors found a way out of the Cesspool Cell and the House of Rex, they had nowhere to go. They heard rumors about the powers of the Astralsauruses, but they had no reason to think that they would help them. After all, the Astralsauruses were one of the key factors in securing the Tyrannosaurus Rex's domination."

"Wait," Emma suspiciously interrupted, squeezing her leafy chair every other second, "how did they escape?"

"Silence!" an Apatosaurus shouted who lay beside Reggie. "Speak not and respect the prophecy!"

"As I was saying," Reggie said, "our ancestors escaped on a pirate ship. Years had passed since they'd seen the sun, and gaining another glimpse of its beaming beauty became their sole objective. One day, delirious from being underfed and overworked, they saw an image of Bau as they prepared to let their most recently finished pirate ship sail down the stream connecting the Cesspool Cell to the plateau above the House of Rex. Bau's face had replaced the Piratops figurehead, which they had constructed the day before. Some of the Apatosauruses took this as a sign from Bau, signaling safe passage out of the House of Rex, and they boarded the ship. Others took this as a delirium-induced hallucination, insisting that they would never survive the geyser leading to the River of Rex, reminding all of our ancestors that only a small portion of the ships they made actually survived the ascent. But those who left on the ship survived. And those who stayed behind were executed a day later, when the Tyrannosaurus Rex learned from his Task Force that the Apatosauruses who escaped had survived the geyser's ejaculation."

"And what about the Astralsauruses?" Throughout all his research, Colin had never heard of this species. "What do they look like? How did they help?"

Reggie sighed and moved his neck in wide circles, as if rolling his whole head, instead of his eyes, were the only way he could convey his annoyance. "We don't know their true appearance. Our ancestors only saw their Earth form. But as the escaped Apatosauruses sailed the pirate ship down the River of Rex, the Tyrannosaurus Task Force discovered them. In fear of being returned to the House of Rex, they abandoned ship and danced into the Arium of the Astralsaurus. After a few hours of aimless wandering, our species had been captured once again, this time by the Astralsauruses. For a couple of days they lived in underground prisons. There were no lights beneath the Astralsauruses' homes, and in many cases, no food. It was like being back in the Cesspool Cell again, only without the labor and the wetness. And after the first twenty-four hours, most of the Apatosauruses started to hallucinate.

"On the morning of the third day," Reggie continued, "the cellar doors were opened, and all the Apatosauruses rose out of the darkness and into the day's first sun prisms. The Astralsauruses led our ancestors to the center of their Arium, and once they arrived, they prophesized the coming of Bau.

"They said, 'You are to build a Brontosaurus pirate ship, which alien dancers from the future will one day discover hidden in an ice cave. When they arrive, the aliens must defeat your most talented dancers in a dance-off. If they succeed, you will equip them with a guide to lead them to the House of Rex where these strange futuristic dancers will challenge the Tyrannosaurus Rex to his Ultimate Dinosaur Dance-Off. If they come out victorious, they will bring Bau back down to Earth, who will in turn save dinosaurkind from extinction. But until that day comes, you will no longer live in this world. We have created an Astral in a dimension lying between this one and the plane, and in it you will wait. And know this: We have also passed a small portion of our powers onto you, and with it, you can access your Astral at two points. The first entrance is located at the northernmost point of the Northern Plains, near the field of grass on the edge of the island, and the second entrance is in the center of the Days of the Dinosaur. Your Astral can only be reached by visitors if one of your species accompanies them. Everyone else will dance through the north half of this island without realizing they are on the verge of another dimension. Now go find the central entrance and wait in your Astral until you receive the sign.' You, Colin and Emma," Reggie said, enraptured, "are our sign."

Colin wanted to preserve the prophecy by giving it time to dissolve into his mind. Could he really be their sign? Could he actually be the Apatosaurus savior? But the second Reggie stopped speaking, the mushroom absorbed their leafy seats, returning them to its cap. A rocket exploded overhead, sending confetti down from the crystallized grass sky, causing Wolfmother's "Dimension" to ring throughout the Astral of the Apatosaurus. Before Colin could truly comprehend what had happened, Rose had placed her tail in his hand, and Emma's hands had landed on his back, and nothing else mattered. His dream dinosaur led him in their conga-line once more. Subconsciously, his mind wandered back to his psychedelic swing with Rose. He recreated the night they met so that instead of slow dancing themselves to sleep, they slow danced themselves into an intertwined hug. All the other animals slept. But as they lay there under the blinking stars, Rose pushed Colin away from her. She bit the button off his jeans. She pinched the zipper between her teeth.

"Why didn't they say anything about Joe?" Emma pressed her lips against Colin's ears as she shouted directly into his drum. "Their prophecy said a bunch of shit about futuristic dancers saving them, but they never said that one of the saviors would need saving, too."

The dance had dragged them across the bridge and through the audience house on the other side. Now they retraced their steps down the zigzag path. Over his shoulder, Colin shouted, "Rose said he'll be fine, and we've been able to trust her so far."

"Why didn't they say anything about Joe?"

"Maybe they thought that part of the prophecy would be obvious to us?"

"Their prophecy said a bunch of shit about futuristic dancers saving them…"

Colin could hardly hear her, and he felt her lips moving uncomfortably along his ear as she shouted. It dawned on him that Emma could not have possibly heard anything he said because he faced away from her. Without being able to hear him, she must have thought that the words failed to flow both ways. She kept on yelling louder and louder until her words became a mantra in Colin's mind: "Why didn't they say anything about Joe?"

When they entered the food house, Rose wavered from the walkway, leading the conga-line down the dark dinosaur hole. The music's volume increased significantly as the sounds reverberated around the tube; Colin couldn't hear his own screams. Despite their descent, after falling a few hundred feet, he calmed himself enough to focus on his surroundings.

Colorful cupboards coated the interior of the dinosaur hole, and as they continued their descent, Colin realized that Rose and Emma were digging through the shelves, gathering an array of vegetables. Suddenly, his stomach bubbled, and he felt like a tar pit devoid of fossils. He reached for the closest cupboard, a red one, and found tomatoes inside. Below it, he stuck his hand into a maroon cabinet, retrieving a pair of beets. The cupboards then turned different shades of purple, and Colin collected eggplants, cabbages, and kale. After falling past the entire rainbow of vegetables again and again, and after he had stuffed his clothes with plants as if they were pockets, he felt his body slip into an unlit chute. While he slid along the slide's wooden surface, he realized that the chute probably carried him across the top of the ceiling above the lowest house in the Astral of the Apatosaurus. The cave paintings popped into his mind, but this time he saw himself receiving the award in the last image of the last dance-off series.

Colin slid down the chute for what seemed like hours. But since surpassing the tree house, he had forgotten about the paintings. Thoughts of Rose replaced the art as he slid into the darkness behind her. And as he held her tail in his hands, he let the music move him out of the Apatosauruses' dimension and into the Days of the Dinosaur.

The Pact (Chapter Eleven)

By the time Colin stepped into the hospital's waiting room, Emma had already blown through a box of tissues, which were piled on the chair beside her. He scanned the room for a trashcan, found one on the floor before the receptionist's window, and carried it to where Emma wilted. He used the crook of his arm to drag the tissue mountain from the chair to the can, and once it had been cleared, he sat by her side.

"How is he?" Colin reached out an arm and wrapped it around Emma, and Moby Grape's "It's a Beautiful Day Today" played softly overhead.

"He's in emergency surgery. He ruptured his spleen and punctured a lung. They said he has severe internal bleeding and that he's lucky to be alive."

"But will he survive?"

"The doctors are optimistic. They said he would."

"That's great," Colin said, exhaling. He still couldn't believe Joe had actually attempted it. Sure, he danced amazingly, but that didn't mean he could master the move that killed their mother. The Grand Break was impossible.

"Yeah," Emma said, nodding, "I know. I just wish I would've stopped him before he stepped on stage. As we were walking to the gym, I begged him to do a different dance for the talent show, but I knew he wasn't going to listen. I could see it in his eyes.

And yes, he's alive, and I'm so happy, but they said he'd likely lose his spleen. And now if he gets sick, he can die. And all because I didn't stop him." Another tissue mountain grew on her lap. "I'm just so scared of losing him. Since I failed to save my family, he's all I have, and I don't know what I'd do." She stopped and sobbed.

Colin hugged her and wanted to tell her that no matter what happened, she couldn't have changed Joe's stubborn mind. Similar to her familial fiasco, she bore no fault. But Emma had never believed his protests in the past, so instead, he simply said, "Joe wouldn't let that happen, not after all you've been through the last few months."

Up until she graduated high school, Emma had been a part of the Young Equestrian League. But when she started college, because of the school's strict dormitory policy banning pets, she had to leave her prized horse, Bentley, behind. Apparently, while Emma had been at school the last three and a half semesters, her mother had started cheating on her father with Emma's favorite horse. She knew this because three months ago, after her father had discovered the affair, he shot his wife and his daughter's beloved horse before pulling the gun on himself. Emma had yet to forgive herself for leaving her darling horse with her family.

Without a home to return to, she had stayed with us over spring break, and planned to stay with us again over the summer in a few weeks. Of course, she had a few dance friends at school that she could theoretically stay with if Joe succumbed to the Grand Break, but because she had spent so much time with her boyfriend, none of her other friends were particularly close. She had Colin, too, but he didn't think she'd want to hang around him if Joe were missing from the equation. "Don't worry," he said, looking into her bright blue eyes, "he's strong. If he can survive the Grand Break, bacteria won't pose any problems."

"Yeah, he is," Emma agreed, grinning. "But he's overly adventurous, too. We'll have to try to keep him from getting sick, and if he does, we'll have to take care of him. And we can never let him try the Grand Break again."

"Deal," Colin said, continuing to marvel at how his brother had survived the impossible.

"Promise?"

"Promise," he said. "If Joe loses his spleen, then I'll take special care of him when he's sick. And if he ever decides to try the Grand Break again, I'll do whatever it takes to stop him, even if that means knocking him unconscious."

"I'd like to see you try," Emma said, smiling slightly, and the streaks down her cheeks started to dry.

Colin returned her smile as they fell silent. Knowing that his brother would survive, he tried to focus on their future camping trips to Fraser River, the Big Four Ice Caves, and Trillium Lake. But again and again, he could only see Joe's body breaking too hard, breaking into blood, and then his brother transformed into his mother, and Colin saw himself as a child sitting in the private balcony box closest to the stage, watching her, his hero, dance in front of thousands, and then she screamed louder than she'd ever screamed before, and blood started to stain her white leotard, and then she went silent, and her lower body, balanced above her head, slowly slid off her upper body, and she thumped down to the floor, and before he understood what had happened, his dad had taken his hand and led him through the red curtains and away from the auditorium. And in that moment, he wished he had been the one stuck at home with the flu instead of Joe.

Emma blew her nose. Colin shook the memory away. Overhead, he heard Ultimate Spinach's "[Ballad of] the Hip Death Goddess." He shivered, and the door to the waiting room swung open. A doctor approached.

"How is he?" Emma asked, standing.

"Joe's going to be okay," the doctor said. "We had to remove his spleen, but he'll make a full recovery. He will have to pay close attention to infections for the rest of his life. And if he ever leaves the country, he'll have to bring antibiotics with him as a precaution. But other than that, in about six weeks' time, he should be back to normal."

"Thank you," Colin said, stunned that in a month and a half, Joe would make a full recovery from his Grand Break.

"Can we see him?" Emma asked.

"This way," the doctor said, extending her arm toward the door as she walked toward it.

62

The Tyrannosaurus Task Force (Chapter Twelve)

THE HUMIDITY AND HEAT HIT COLIN the second he shot out of the chute, as if he had slid into a sauna. He was falling. His stomach fluttered above him, hot wind stabbed his eyes, and darkness surrounded him. He heard a simultaneous crash and crunch as he slammed against the crystallized grass, though he didn't feel any pain. Instead, he felt tranquil as he lay there in the dark.

Slowly, the darkness grew a few shades lighter as his eyes adjusted, and he started to perceive the outlines of the smaller trees as they waved, waltzing beneath ancestral shadows. A sudden burst of brightness shimmied across the sky, but before Colin could spy the chute from which he fell, the starlight fizzled back to black. His eyes had to readjust to the darkness, and once they had, another star shot through the sky. Colin scanned the treetops, searching for the hole that he slid through, but all the treetops looked the same, and from there he moved to the empty space above, hoping to uncover a tear in the dark fabric of sky. He failed to find anything, and as the darkness resettled, his stomach snarled. This process repeated itself a few more times before Colin accepted the chute's opening had disappeared. As the light dimmed, his stomach growled again. And as he stuck a hand down his pants to retrieve a cucumber, he realized that stuffing his clothes with vegetables had cushioned his fall and saved his life.

Once he had swallowed the last of his appetizer, he fished out a head of cabbage from just below the back of his neck and continued to eat. But before he could chew it down to its last leaf, T. Rex's "Cosmic Dancer" blew by in the breeze. Colin leapt to his feet and immediately began to dance. He did the reverse shopping cart, pulling vegetables out of his clothes and shoving them into his mouth. He spotted Emma doing a wonderful worm, but he couldn't find Rose anywhere. Maybe she had gotten lost somewhere in the chute? Maybe she had ditched them in there so she could go back to her Astral and rid herself of him? Colin's reverse shopping cart became bumpy.

But a few chords before the climax of "Cosmic Dancer," Rose surged from the shrubbery, sweeping Colin and Emma into the bushes in a single motion.

"That fucking hurt," Emma said, "and you ruined our jam."

Rose's face wavered between fury and fright. At first, Colin worried that his ridiculous dance had upset her, and he was sick with sweat. But Rose's face changed, and her new expression scared him.

"Don't move," she hissed.

Colin nodded slightly, his head never raising enough to meet Rose's eyes. He heard Emma intervene. She asked, "Why?"

Rose wrapped her tail around Emma's face, coiling her mouth closed. "That song," she whispered, "it's the Tyrannosaurus Task Force's theme song. Whenever it plays, you know the Velociraptors are near."

When Emma tried to respond, her words turned to senseless sounds as they sifted through Rose's spiraling tail.

The song's volume increased and the scent of cinnamon wafted through the air. A shiver ran along Colin's spine, cooling the sweat on his back. Even though science had shown Velociraptors to be no larger than a small turkey, and similarly covered in feathers, he stressed about the ways the Tyrannosaurus Rex could have genetically modified his Task Force. The images of the Utahraptor-based Velociraptors from *Jurassic Park* kept on carouseling around his mind. He envisioned the human-sized beasts with their reptilian flesh, and he could only picture their terrible claws ripping the three of them apart.

"See them," Rose said, as light started to seep through the trees, and she motioned toward the glow with her tail.

The cinnamon scent increased, and Colin exhaled. Two Velociraptors had danced into the starlight from the shade of a tree. They were the size of modest chickens. And as far as Colin could tell, their only modifications were that they smelled like cinnamon and glowed.

"We're hiding from those things?" Emma asked.

"Yes," Rose said. "Those are just the scouts. The rest will arrive soon."

Emma sighed, but before she could object, "Cosmic Dancer" had climaxed, and the trees behind the two tiny dinosaurs began to arch, their middles expanding horizontally while their tips prepared to touch. The front line of the Tyrannosaurus Task Force floated into view through the improvised aperture. They stretched twenty raptors wide, and once they passed through the opening, the trees returned to their upright positions, closing their passageway as they resumed their wavy dance. This process repeated itself until ten rows of Velociraptors had floated through the recurring gap in the trees.

The raptors carried a coat of glowing, neon green plumage striped by inconsistent yellow streaks, and they sported blue beaks. Their movements defied any modern hypotheses, too. While Colin no longer expected them to walk, he supposed that they would at least be grooving along the ground. But as he observed them pass through the portal, he realized they moved in loose levitation, some dinosaurs floating a few feet above the grass while others hovered a half-dozen inches. Moreover, they progressed in glitches, as if they were dancing through a flipbook. In this manner the Tyrannosaurus Task Force moved throughout the forest, and the moment they disappeared, "Cosmic Dancer" came to a close.

"The Tyrannosaurus Rex only genetically modified the Velociraptors so they would glow and levitate?" Colin stood and resumed his reverse shopping cart, bringing a fistful of Brussels sprouts to his mouth. "How did that help him overthrow the Days of the Dinosaur?"

"It didn't," Rose said, still lying on the ground. "The Tyrannosaurus Task Force wasn't created to overthrow anything. They were devised to dance. Their glow is just for flare, but their levitation allows them to move in ways that were previously impossible when they were still plagued by gravity."

Emma said, "You mean, aside from dancing, they're powerless?"

"Yeah, more or less," Rose said.

"Then why haven't the Apatosauruses wiped out the Tyrannosaurus Task Force already? I mean, how could you just fucking let them take Joe?"

"Enough, Emma."

"Enough of what?" Emma responded.

"Blaming Rose," Colin continued. "Blaming the Apatosauruses. They're doing everything they can to help us. We all want him back."

"Bullshit," she cried. "Why didn't you stop the Velociraptors from capturing Joe when you saw them dance away with him?"

Rose sighed and said, "Because it's forbidden."

Emma let loose a lemony laugh.

Rose said, "Even if I had attacked the Velociraptors on my own, even if I had rescued Joe, some of the Task Force would have surely escaped and alerted the Tyrannosaurus Rex that the Apatosauruses are still alive, which would endanger us all."

Naptime (Chapter Thirteen)

COLIN DANCED THROUGH THE FOREST, propelling his legs into the air as he leapt from foot to foot. While airborne, he pointed one foot at the inside of his other leg, always leading his *pas de chat* with his left. Emma moved along the crystallized grass through windmills, using her hands to spin her body from her back to her belly again and again, legs flailing through the air. And Rose travelled by the strangest jumpstyle Colin had ever seen. She techno jumped from her front to hind legs, twirling in circles every few steps. Together, they danced in the darkness to Canned Heat's "Going Up the Country," their path lighted in strobes by the pulsating moon.

All the trees looked the same, and as they blurred into each other, creating the mirage of two massive rainbow walls, Colin started to lose track of time under the airy tunnel of Canned Heat. He wondered how Joe had been getting along with the Tyrannosaurus Task Force as a guide, and if he enjoyed dancing with dinosaurs despite his circumstances. Colin spent a lot of energy sending Joe positive vibes as he created a scenario where his brother would be having a good time. He imagined Joe levitating along the ground with the Velociraptors, but then the rustling of water interrupted him, and Colin thought about his thirst. He imagined how thirsty Joe must be, and he realized how incredibly stupid his fantasy had been of his brother having fun.

After all, Joe couldn't levitate. And even if he could, the Tyrannosaurus Task Force probably had him chained.

Rose took a few techno steps in front of Colin and Emma, and using her tail to signal them, she led them toward the sounds of stirring water. After Colin performed a few more *pas de chats*, the tunnel of trees opened up to a linear clearing, and in its center sat the Big River. It appeared to be as wide as a mega-Apatosaurus is long, but Colin lacked confidence in what he perceived. He guessed its size probably equaled that of a suburban street. He left Emma and Rose along the tree line as he danced toward the water's edge and collapsed to his knees. Cupping his hands, Colin drank cold puddles.

As he drained cup after cup, Emma asked the Apatosaurus about the plants.

"Rose," she said, standing into a two-step before lifting a rainbow-shaded leaf from a dangling branch, "why are all the bushes and trees on the island so colorful?" The dinosaur leaned her head to her left. "I mean, where I'm from, when plants have vibrant pigments, it's usually so that insects and other animals will eat them, and in doing so, spread their seed. But the only animals I've seen on the island have been dinosaurs, and none of them have eaten the plants."

"We eat the leaves from time to time," Rose said, "usually when we're away from our Astral without food. But their color has nothing to do with our diet. Almost everything on the island is vibrant like the plants because color is the symbol of life."

"But the plants couldn't have always resembled rainbows," Emma protested. "It has to be some sort of survival tactic, right?"

Rose tilted her snout toward the sky, shrugging. "Our island has been overflowing with color ever since dinosaurs first danced. It's even possible that the color existed before the day the Earth shook. No animal actually knows the origin of the rainbow."

"Fascinating," Emma said, dropping the leaf in her hand and two-stepping toward the Big River. "I wish we had plants like this where I'm from. They're more lively than the loveliest of flowers."

Colin began to feel bloated as Rose and Emma joined him by the riverside, and he leaned up and fell onto his back. He pulled a couple of tomatoes out of the front of his pants and slowly began to eat. He felt the tomatoes turn into sofas between his teeth, and he got lost in comfort as he chewed on the soft red cushions. After he finished, he threw the stems into the river, and he noticed that Rose watched him. Emma looked lost in her own way, staring down the river, water stirring in her eyes.

"We should get some rest," Rose said.

Emma didn't react. Colin didn't react either even though he tried.

"Tomorrow will be a long and dangerous day," Rose said. "We will need all the sleep we can get."

Rose bit the front of Colin's shirt, dragging him to his feet. Once standing, Colin couldn't help but *pas de chat* in place despite his protests. He danced all the pleasure out of his body, and then Rose motioned to Emma. Colin shook his head. Rose insisted. So he grabbed his friend under her arms and lifted her to her feet. Her lack of resistance surprised him. On her feet, Emma half-heartedly two-stepped.

"Follow me." Rose jumpstyled back toward the forest. "If the Tyrannosaurus Task Force wanders by," she said, breaking the barrier of the tree wall mirage, "they won't be able to see us in here. We'll be safe unless they happen to travel between the exact trees beneath which we sleep."

Colin danced behind the dinosaur until they found a spot to settle down. Besides Rose, who stood within hug distance, Colin could only see the blurred wall of trees in every direction. He had no idea which way the tree tunnel waited. He couldn't even remember how to return to the river. As he *pas de chatted* in circles, trying to chart his coordinates, he failed to find Emma everywhere he looked.

"Wait here." Rose disappeared into the mirage. And then Colin heard her voice floating from the other side, saying, "I'm going to fetch Emma. Be back soon. Relax and get some rest."

Colin tried to sleep, but the second he closed his eyes he saw Rose abandoning him in the forest, returning to her Apatosaurus boyfriend. Colin imagined them twisting their tails, licking each other's lips, and the darkness from the neon-purple dance floor began to creep back in. Every second since Rose had departed seemed like an hour, and eventually, a day, a week. Colin felt as if his whole body consisted of shadows. The scent of amber incense, the surface of the crystallized grass below his back, the palms of his hands, and even the oxygen felt as if they were photocopies. His entire existence boiled down to the darkness he dwelled in. Then the black swallowed Colin and he sailed into sleep.

—

Rose's voice dragged Colin out of his darkness. She shook his legs with her tail and whispered into his ear, "Colin, wake up."

At first, Colin kicked the tail away. Then, he groggily realized a dinosaur pulled at his legs. Still believing Rose had abandoned him, he shot up to his feet and prepared to sprint to safety. But when he stood, he struggled to find enough energy to do a sleepy, singular square dance.

"Get down," Rose hissed, "you'll wake Emma."

"Rose!" Colin cried, square dancing.

"Quiet," Rose whispered. She swept Colin off his feet with her tail, catching him with her neck before he crashed against the crystallized grass.

"But what about your boyfriend?" Colin asked. He couldn't believe Rose had returned as she cradled him.

"What?" Rose's neck formed a quivering question mark.

"Nothing," Colin said, trying to regain his cool as he swiped the sleep from his eyes. Looking around, he realized the deepest layer of darkness had been peeled back, and soon the sun would begin to rise. "Is it time to get going again?" Colin let a yawn slip past his lips.

"Not yet." She set Colin down and slid her tail into his hand. "I just wanted to spend some time alone with you before we start our day."

"Really?" Colin pinched his arm. Felt pain.

"Yes," Rose said, sliding her tail further into Colin's hand. He could no longer close his fist around it. "You're not like any of the other futuristic dancers I've met. Something's different. I don't know what it is yet, but I'll find it."

Colin wanted to tell Rose it was because he loved her, because he desired her dinosaur flesh and had since boyhood. Instead, he just said, "You're really here," and smiled.

"Tell me Colin," Rose said, tilting her head slightly to the side, her face hovering within kiss distance, "what dance do you plan to use to defeat the Tyrannosaurus Rex?"

"Uh." He had no idea. He gave her the first dance that came to mind. "Salsa."

"Salsa," Rose said. "What's that?"

"It's hard to explain."

"Well, then will you show me?"

"Yes." Colin almost shouted his response, but felt relieved that he kept himself under relative control. Surely, if he had shouted, he would have totally killed the mood. Rose's face now hovered so close to his that their cheeks practically touched, and their mouths were pressed against each other's ears. Aroused, he bit his lip hard. Again, felt pain. He told himself to keep cool. That this wasn't a big deal. Rose had simply agreed to a basic salsa lesson. And that's when he realized he didn't exactly know how to salsa. "It's easy," Colin said, more to himself than Rose.

"Great." Rose grinned.

"You're so goddamn gorgeous!" Colin meant to say beautiful. Meant to exclude the goddamn.

"Thanks," Rose said. Her smile stayed put, and Colin exhaled.

"First step is to stand." Colin stood with Rose's tail in his right hand. He reached for Rose's head with his left. Colin told himself that so far he had nailed it.

"Like this?" Rose asked, standing.

"Exactly," Colin said. "That's perfect."

"So what's next?"

"Next, of course!" Colin thought Rose was so smart. "Uh," he said, "follow my lead?"

"I'm all yours," Rose said, looking at Colin intently.

Colin took a few deep breaths. He cursed his hands for sweating, almost apologized about it, but he didn't want to draw more attention to it. Then he brought Rose into the closed position, placing her tail on his shoulder while unsuccessfully trying to wrap his right hand around her body. He quickly discovered he couldn't even reach her butt, never mind her other side. Pushing Rose away gently, he grabbed her tail again, and reverted back to the open position.

"You move your feet like this," Colin said, shifting his weight from side to side, humming sounds that resembled a slower paced version of the salsa.

"Is this right?" Rose asked, alternating her weight between her front and hind legs.

"Exactly." Colin could not believe how quickly Rose caught on. "Now let's try something a little more complex."

He let go of Rose's head and spun himself in a circle as he held her tail. He ended up standing beside her, and he continued shifting his weight back and forth, swinging the dinosaur's tail as they danced. He smiled at Rose and she returned the gesture, but she looked pained. Colin followed her eyes and found her tail, and he realized he hadn't loosened his grip when he spun around, and now the scales around his hand were twisted tight. They turned red, as if he had snake bit her arm. "Shoot, sorry!" Colin said.

Trying to fix his mistake, Colin lifted Rose's tail and twirled her around. But considering the length of his arm, he created a space significantly too small for the Apatosaurus's body to spin through. Colin realized this when Rose had made it halfway through her swing, when her neck and upper body crashed into him. Already off-balance because of her rotation, when she hit the unexpected weight in her way, the front of Rose's body slowed down, and her momentum caused her to sprawl out on the floor on top of Colin.

He heard someone clapping slowly. Then he felt the weight being withdrawn as Rose lifted herself up, stepping into an involuntary, upbeat shimmy. As Colin stood and started a stiff two-step, he saw that Emma had sat up and smiled.

"Smooth," she said. She continued to clap.

"Are you okay?" Rose rubbed his stomach with her head. "I'm so sorry."

"Never been better," Colin lied. "And I'm the one who should be sorry. I'm such a lousy lead."

"Nonsense, you did great," Rose said, returning the deceit. She used her tail to wipe his hair out of his eyes as she massaged his chest with her closed mouth.

"Do you mean it?" Colin asked.

"It was nice," Rose said, nestling her nose into his neck. "I really liked it."

Rose continued to raise her head until her mouth rested on Colin's chin. Just before their lips met, she turned around and tap-danced through the tree wall mirage.

"Having fun?" Emma asked.

"Yeah," Colin said, carelessly.

"I'm sure your brother's having a blast right now, too."

"I want him back, Emma. I'm worried about him as well. I'm just trying to make the best of the situation."

"Well stop dicking around. Let's go save him already."

"Deal!" Colin's eyes became crescent-shaped and he showed Emma his teeth, hoping to help her feel at ease. She just turned around and tap-danced after Rose. Colin followed her, tap dancing out of the forest to the edge of the river.

Rose had already moved a whole mushroom dance-floor downstream. Colin hurried his tap dance, imagining he and Emma were racing to Rose. He lost. But once he grooved by the dinosaur's side, tap dancing with her tail in his hand as the sun rose before them, he felt fine.

The stream seemed to stir up some music, and Quicksilver Messenger Service's "Fresh Air" spilled into the atmosphere. And as they tap danced into the distance, the smiling sun began to sing.

Colin and the Paleoartist (Chapter Fourteen)

COLIN BECAME SEXUALLY AROUSED for the first time at age nine. He went to a museum in Chicago with Joe and their dad, and as they entered the main gallery, a huge, open hall, he spotted her. She stood on the far side of the airy space, looking directly at him, as if she'd been waiting for him ever since her installation. Her plaque called her Sue, and she was the largest, best-preserved, and most complete Tyrannosaurus Rex fossil ever found.

Colin and his family closed the distance between him and his first crush, and he started whistling the Rolling Stones' "She's a Rainbow." Colin wanted to ditch his family to experience this moment without them, but he feared repercussions. He wanted to understand why his hands had suddenly started to sweat, why his stomach felt upside-down, and why a halo had surrounded the dinosaur's skeleton. But more than any of that, Colin wished he were completely alone with this fossil, rubbing his hands over the surface of Sue's beautiful body. His blood had rushed to the edge of his every extremity, and he felt all the eyes in the museum's main hall starring at him hard. He thought about how his dad had loved his mom before she died, and he knew these feelings toward Sue were abnormal. He began to cry.

"What's wrong?" his dad asked.

"Nothing," he said, wiping away the tears with the sleeve of his sweater. "I just miss Mom."

Joe rolled his eyes.

"Me too, kid. Me too." His father audibly exhaled. Pointing at the dinosaur, he added, "But can you believe the size of this thing? Can you even imagine how big Sue would have been with her feathers and flesh?"

"Yeah," Colin said, the tears now nothing more than a memory. But he wished he could convey to his father that he saw Sue in her living form. He pictured the Tyrannosaurus Rex alone in the woods as they continued their trek across the museum hall. Spear-tipped braches had cut both her legs while she charged another dinosaur, maybe a smaller theropod or an ornithopod, which she had failed to catch for dinner. She asked Colin to come close to her, to kiss her cuts until the pain fled. He nodded, wetting his lips. The few feet between them swiftly shrank to inches, and he stretched out his arms, puckered his lips.

His father yanked his hand, dragging him down from the barred fence separating Sue from the visitors, pulling Colin out of his fantasy.

"What's with you today?" his dad asked, more curious than critical.

"He's in love," Joe said, laughing.

Their dad shot Joe a hard stare.

"I'm sorry, dad," Colin said, unable to take his eyes off Sue. "This fossil is just so," he chose his next word carefully, "cool."

"She sure is, Colin." The man grabbed the pencil in his back pocket. In his other hand, he held a sketchbook. "Mind waiting here and watching Sue for a few minutes? I'm going to go sit on the bench over there," he motioned to the dinosaur's left with his head, "to draft a few different outlines for my next painting."

"Can I come with you?" Joe asked. "This is boring. And I don't want to interrupt Colin and his girlfriend."

"Yeah, I guess," their dad said, sighing. "Just don't make any noise."

Colin ignored his brother's insult and his grin grew.

"We'll be right over there. I'll see everything you do," his father's face sported a stern expression, "so don't you even think about climbing the barrier again. Understand?"

"Yes, dad," Colin said.

"Good," he said, and he walked toward the bench with Joe to

begin sketching "King Carnivore," the next piece in his collection on carnivorous dinosaurs.

Alone, Colin stared up into Sue's massive face. He studied the curvature of her jaw line, her long, skinny teeth, and the hollowed out holes where her ferocious eyes once rested. Something about the length of her horizontal head especially excited him, but he couldn't find the words to describe it. Ogling the dinosaur's colossal cranium, Colin dreamed about kissing Sue, and then he desired more.

The Dance of the Discodactyl (Chapter Fifteen)

AN ANXIETY ATTACK temporarily incapacitated Colin. Before the attack, Rose led him in a jitterbug through the forest while Emma did a wilting waltz behind them. Colin had just started to get the hang of the dance when the attack hit, interrupting his dreams of jitterbugging with Rose in their private tree house.

The anxiety attached itself to a tree on the other side of the stream. The tree's leafy brain morphed into his father's face, and the trunk below it turned into his neck. As Rose led him in their jitterbug, and he became more parallel with the tree of his father, the neck turned so they could maintain eye contact. When he danced directly across from his father's rainbow face, the tree spoke to him. It said, "Son, I see you're still dancing," and Colin froze.

"What the heck?" he said, tipping over, falling to the floor. "You're here?"

"Years ago," the tree said, "you promised me you wouldn't risk hurting yourself by dance. And now look at the dangers dancing has brought you."

"I'm sorry," Colin said to the tree. "I know it hurts you to see me like this."

"It infuriates me!" the tree shouted, some of its leaves shedding as it shook. Its branches then curved toward the ground, causing his father's whole face to transform into a frown. The leaves burned red. "Son," the tree said, sounding tired, "I'm just so disappointed. First your brother nearly kills himself by attempting to execute the Grand Break, trying to recreate the great, late Victoria Warby's death. And I refuse to experience that pain again. I hope you can see why I had to disown him even though I love him."

"I know," Colin picked his words carefully, refusing to bite his dad's bait in regard to Joe, "and I understand the fear that mom's death instilled is why you told me you wouldn't waste a dollar on dance after you found out I got into both the geology and dance programs at school."

"Another disappointment," the tree added.

"But," Colin continued, staying strong, "I can't avoid dancing any longer. I need to feel close to mom again."

The tree laughed coldly. It said, "If you think dancing will reunite you with your mother, then not only do you disappoint me, you're also an idiot."

"It will work," Colin said, hurt by the tree's words.

"Of course it will," the tree said, mocking Colin with comfort. "If by reuniting with your mother, you mean meeting her in the afterlife. If you continue dancing, know you're no better than your brother, know you're no son of mine."

His father's face withered away. Colin shook on the forest floor, looking at the tree, trying to avoid the stare of its leaves.

Rose rested her tail in Colin's hand, and the anxiety of defying his dad with dance slowly dissipated. He tried to resume his jitterbug with Rose, but before she would lead him again, she asked if he had fully recovered from his convulsing episode, asked about what had just happened. Colin shrugged, said he's great as long as he could continue his dance with her. So they did, and a warm, tingling euphoria, which he believed to be the result of Rose's embrace, replaced his anxiety. But when he saw Emma disco dancing in her own euphoric daze a few mushroom dance-floors ahead of them, he knew his happiness came from exterior forces.

Lipps Inc's "Funkytown" began to bounce in the breeze. Colin let go of Rose and turned his jitterbug into a dreamy disco.

"Colin," he heard Rose calling, her voice breaking through the haze. "Watch out for the warmth." Rose pointed toward Emma with her tail. "Don't let that happen."

Colin first noticed the snow. It turned the river to ice and stripped the trees of their multicolored leaves. Lost in euphoria, he had somehow failed to see the fresh powder earlier, which covered everything between him and Emma. Then he really saw Emma. She had lain down, scooping piles of powder into her mouth and burying herself alive.

"It's curious," Colin said to Rose, bending over to touch the ground. "This snow is warm." The desire to copy Emma's actions suddenly swarmed him. The temptation to sit and stay stagnant became unbearable. "Rose," he whispered, "what is this place?"

"The Domain of the Discodactyl," Rose said. "The warmth already has a hold on Emma. You need to keep dancing. If it gets you, too, Emma won't make it."

"But I already feel so warm. So pleasant." Colin could feel himself on the verge of sitting. His knees started to buckle. Rose smacked his face with her tail. She hit him so hard he tipped over. Rose quickly used her tail to bring him back to his feet, but Colin had a cut across his cheek and some powder already entered his wound. The warmth seeped back into his body. This time his legs gave out completely, and he collapsed. Rose coiled her tail around him, and holding him above the ground, she smacked his face again and again, connecting with the cut each time. Eventually, the sting brought Colin out of his daze, only to discover his cheek had been shredded. Rose set him back down on his feet, and blood covered the left side of his face. When he touched his cheek, he could poke his finger through the hole and press it against his tongue. Colin thought about grabbing a handful of snow and spreading it over his cheek, numbing his face with warm euphoria.

"Don't even think about it." Rose saw his eyes narrow in on the ground. "If you put that stuff on your face, I'll tear the skin off your skull."

Colin remained unfazed. His eyes were two shriveled doughnut holes, glazed.

Rose stuck the tip of her tail through the hole in Colin's cheek.

"Ow!" he shouted. He yanked the tail out of his cheek and tried to bite it. Opening his mouth only increased the pain. "Eff," he said, fuming.

"Colin." Rose stared into his eyes. "Snap out of it. You'll be fine."

"What happened?" The hole in his cheek confused Colin as well as the searing laceration it had caused.

"The Discodactyls had a hold on you. So I beat it out."

"Discodactyls?"

Rose stretched her neck toward the sky. Colin looked up and saw three dancing Discodactyls above them. They reminded him of pterodactyls, except the body of each Discodactyl consisted of a revolving disco ball, which they used to reflect the sun's rays all over the snowy ground in an attempt to keep their prey from spotting them. The snow fell in flakes from their noses.

"They're scavengers," Rose said. "They drop snow on their victims, filling them with warmth until they bury themselves in it. Then the Discodactyls wait for their food to suffocate before they dive down and dig them out of the grave."

Colin looked for Emma. He could barely see her head peeking out of the snow. "Rose!" He sounded frantic. "Emma's going to die." He screamed his friend's name, but the word melted in his mouth.

"We still have some time," Rose said. "But Colin, I need you to be honest. Are you ready? We can wait a little longer if the temptation has become more present than the pain."

"Let's go," Colin said, disco dancing toward Emma. Rose caught up to him within a few strides. And as they got closer to Emma's grave, the volume of "Funkytown" and the welcoming warmth increased dramatically. If it hadn't been for Rose's tail looming over the hole in Colin's cheek, he would have cannonballed into the celestial powder.

"I'm going to dance up ahead," Rose shouted over the song, "to start digging Emma out of the snow."

Colin nodded.

"When she's out, I need you to storm in and tackle her."

"Let's do it."

"Colin," Rose looked at him, waiting for his eyes, "this is incredibly important. When you tackle her, make sure you land on her. If your momentum rolls you off into the snow, the warmth will take hold, and I won't be able to save both of you. Understand?"

"Completely."

"Good," Rose broke their visual connection, "after you tackle her, after you knock her to her senses, get right back up again and don't stop dancing until you reach the other side of the snow."

"And Emma?"

"I'll take care of Emma. You just worry about yourself."

Rose disco danced in long strides, and before Colin had progressed fifteen feet, the Apatosaurus had grooved the length of a mushroom dance-floor. She used her tail to sweep the snow off Emma's body. Colin quickened the pace of his disco, practically running as he stepped twice to his right and then twice to his left. Whenever he stepped right, he threw that arm into the air diagonally and placed his left hand on his hip with his elbow out. Whenever he stepped left, he repeated the process, reversing the role of his limbs. And as he danced across the Domain of the Discodactyl, now halfway to his friends, he saw that Rose had cleared away all the snow above Emma's thighs.

Colin began to meditate on the moves he would make as he neared them. He envisioned himself diving through the air fully extended as he crashed into Emma's warm body. He thought of different ways he could keep himself from tumbling off her as they fell, and he decided the best action to take would be to grab Emma and hold on as tight as possible. This way, when he tackled her, she would play the part of a heating pad as they slid along the surface, protecting him from the snow. As Rose finished clearing the powder off Emma's body, the dinosaur clenched the girl's sandy blonde hair in her teeth and lifted her to her feet. Colin almost danced within high-five distance when he dove.

The moment he left his feet, Colin realized just how severely he had underestimated the timing of his dive. He had hardly stretched his arms in front of his head before he made contact, and the rest of his body had reached nothing resembling full extension. Instead of hitting her mid torso as he had planned, he crashed into Emma's neck. The coldness of her flesh shocked him, and the instant he touched it, his hands started to burn, as if her flesh were dry ice.

Luckily for Emma, Rose realized how off-target Colin's dive had been, and after he bounced off her body, before he tumbled into the snow, the Apatosaurus bent her neck and caught Colin with her head. He squeezed her tightly, and without thinking, he kissed her snout. Once he realized what he had done, his eyes widened, mortified. But then he saw a smile spread over Rose's face. She killed it quickly and tried to replace it with an annoyance aimed at his poorly timed dive. But Colin didn't believe it.

"Dance out of the snow as fast as you can," Rose said, setting Colin down. "Groove faster than you've ever grooved before."

"Nice catch," Colin said, trying to shake off the chill of Emma's skin.

As he disco danced toward the other side of the Domain of the Discodactyl, the cold constantly increased. Every step sent icicles racing up his body, and he wondered if he were dancing across a sea of cold needles instead of the powder he perceived. His entire body burned, like being in a dry ice bath. And the hole in his cheek prickled with frostbite. The desire to cover himself with warmth became unbearable. He imagined himself tripping, faceplanting into the snow, his body floating in euphoria. Colin continued to fight the cold. Even when he looked at his arms and saw that they were ice cubes, and envisioned his entire body as nothing but differently sized blocks of ice, he kept disco dancing.

And then his body tingled with warmth. At first, Colin thought he had surpassed the last stages of superficial frostbite. He prepared to lose all sensation in his limbs. To test his deterioration, Colin simultaneously bit his lower lip and punched his already tattered cheek. He expected to feel nothing, numbed by the cold. Instead, his face felt like fire had consumed it as the blood from his lip coalesced with the blood pouring in from his cheek, and the size of the hole increased. Once the pain became relatively manageable, he looked around and realized that he disco danced on grass. The river beside him began to thaw, and the trees before him were teeming with color. The trunks of the trees were spiral rainbows and the leaves alternated neon colors.

Staring at the foliage, Colin caught his breath. His friends were still stuck in the Domain of the Discodactyl. He turned around and prepared to dance after them, but then he remembered Rose's words. The dinosaur wrestled with Emma as they traversed the white wasteland. And it took all of his self-restraint to sit on the forest's edge and let Rose handle Emma on her own, which seemed to be a struggle even for someone as big as an Apatosaurus.

Emma didn't stop thrashing. Rose held her by the hair with her mouth, her neck outstretched. Dangling, Emma swung her body back and forth, kicking and scratching the dinosaur's neck with all the power her momentum could produce. When they neared the edge, Rose curled the top of her neck and flung Emma to safety. Emma crashed into Colin, and by the time he picked himself back up, Rose danced on the grass beside them.

"Sorry about that." Rose had her neck pressed against her body, moving it in an array of circles to massage the pain away. "If she hit my neck again I would have dropped her. I had to throw her."

"No worries," Colin said, two-stepping. "Let me see your neck."

Rose's skin looked bruised, but he couldn't say for certain because of the way her tie-dye flesh rolled around her body. But in a couple of places, the surface had been beat open, and blood oozed.

"Dang Rose, are you okay?"

"I'm fine." Rose walked around Colin and knelt before Emma, who still lay on the ground. "Help me save her."

"Christ," Colin said, almost inaudible. He knelt with Rose.

Emma struggled through shallow breaths. She had a few minor cuts along her arms and legs. However, her face had been mutilated. Her right cheek had been torn from its center to the corner of her lips. The other cheek had a gash, but it didn't slice all the way through to her gums. Her left eye had been bruised black and she had a few minor cuts across her forehead.

"Colin, dance downstream until you reach the rapids and then veer left into the forest. Find a calamite tree. It's a tree-sized variant of a horsetail plant. Bring me as many branches as you can carry. Quick! It's the only way to save her."

Colin kept staring at Emma. And then he lost consciousness.

The Calamite Forest (Chapter Sixteen)

A DENSE FIELD OF CALAMITE TREES surrounded Colin when he woke up. Water had turned the grass beneath his feet soggy, and warm rain sprinkled his face. He sat and the world began to carousel. Eventually, the dizziness passed. He looked over at Rose, who he assumed attended to Emma. Her front legs were bent, and with her butt raised, sashaying from side to side, she curved her tail until its tip disappeared in front of her. "The Garden of Earthly Delights" by The United States of America reverberated around the circular glade.

Colin stood and did an embarrassing can-can over to Rose. He couldn't lift his leg above his waist during his high kicks. He asked, "How's she doing?" as he danced behind her, watching her butt sway from side to side.

"Great, all healed up." Rose turned to face him. She smiled. "Now she just needs some rest."

Colin seriously doubted Emma's health had improved as much as Rose's voice seemed to suggest. But as the dinosaur sat back on her hind legs, he saw the impossible. The tear in Emma's cheek had been patched back up, and Colin couldn't even see a scar. Her black eye looked normal again, and he failed to find a single scratch on her body.

He glanced at Rose. He scrunched his forehead. He reached his hand up to his cheek and felt his face had been healed as well. "How?" he asked.

"Calamite." Rose used her tail to indicate the turquoise trees surrounding them. "The branches have magical medicinal qualities. When applied correctly, they heal any wound."

"Amazing," Colin said, can-canning toward a tree. He held the branch in his hand. Sniffed it. The tree smelled like soggy socks, which caused him to grimace. "Can we bring some with us?"

"No." Rose did her awkward four-footed two-step over to Colin. "It loses its medicinal properties within minutes of being picked."

"Oh," Colin said, dropping the branch in his hand. He can-canned over to Emma and sat down. He plucked some carrots out of his shirt and chomped. "When can we leave? Emma will be mad if she learns we let her rest while Joe's in danger."

"He's not in danger," Rose said, two-stepping toward Emma, sitting down across from Colin. She crescented her tail around the sleeping body, thrusting its tip into Colin's hand. "He still has two days of luxury before the feast begins. We're the ones in danger, and Emma needs to rest."

"I mean," Colin said, trying not to get sidetracked by Rose's growing interest in him, "Emma will be worried about Joe until she is able to hold him again."

"I see." Rose pulled her tail out of Colin's hand. She used it to brush Emma's cheek. After a few strokes, Emma opened her eyes.

Colin almost wished he could retract his last statement. He didn't know waking Emma would remove Rose's tail from his hand. He couldn't look away from the Apatosaurus when she stroked Emma's cheek. Even when Emma asked, "What happened?" he found it exceedingly strenuous to slant his sight downward.

"You fell under the spell of the Discodactyls," Rose said.

"You almost died," Colin exclaimed.

"Discodactyls?"

"They're awesome," Colin said. "They're scavenger birds with disco ball bodies." Colin used his arms to form a ball. Rose glared at him. "They're pretty terrifying, too," he added. "They drop snow on their prey and it makes them feel warm, euphoric, until they suffocate themselves with it."

"That sounds somewhat familiar."

"Somewhat? You buried—"

"Do you feel well rested?" Rose asked, cutting Colin off.

"Yeah, I feel great." Emma stretched, as if she had come out of an extended coma. "What is this place?" Her pupils were expanding. "I've never seen horsetail with hues of blue before. And they're infinitely bigger than the ones back home."

"They're calamite trees," Colin said, "and they're the only reason we're alive."

"This is the Calamite Forest," Rose added, "and if you're feeling strong enough, we should keep dancing."

Before she got up, Emma said, "Thank you, Rose." She stared at the Apatosaurus. "I don't know what you did back there, but I know that without you, we would never reach the House of Rex." She glanced at the grass. "I'm sorry I've been treating you like shit. It's just, without his antibiotics—"

"Don't mention it," Rose said. "And we haven't made it yet. Let's get moving. There's still a long way to dance."

Colin can-canned in disbelief. He had never heard Emma apologize before. He scarcely knew what had happened when Rose slid her tail into his hand, when Emma placed hers on his shoulders, recreating their conga-line. The dinosaur danced them out of the Calamite Forest to the edge of the river, and they followed the sounds of the water as it stirred downstream.

Prehistoric Pirates (Chapter Seventeen)

COLIN SURMISED THAT IT HAD BEEN A WEEK since they left the Calamite Forest, and consequently, Joe had been eaten. While the sun had yet to set—it burned him badly—they'd been congalining for so long that his feet felt like sand. Maybe, he speculated, the sun had snuck away a number of times over the past week and they were just so focused on their dance that they didn't notice. Or, more likely, the sun orbited the Earth significantly slower in prehistoric times, so even though it hadn't technically set, a week had still passed. He shared his hypotheses with Emma, and despite looking worried, she laughed.

"What's so funny?" Rose asked.

"Colin thinks it has been a week since we saw the Discodactyls."

Rose's snout inflated, and a few seconds later, she laughed, too. "I'm sorry," she said, quickly regaining composure, "it's just, it has only been a few hours. Maybe some more water might help? Sometimes, the sun makes time stretch for us, too, but that's usually after days without water."

Colin nodded, and his face burned even more than before. Rose immediately veered right, cutting through the forest toward the river.

"See?" Emma stuck her tongue out at Colin and blew spit on the back of his neck as their bodies brushed against the rainbow branches.

As the trees became sparser, Colin looked up at the sun, and he had to admit it appeared spectacularly stagnant. It hadn't appeared to move at all since he regained consciousness so long ago. As he let the sky absorb his sight, hypnotized by its dripping shades of rainbow sherbet, sweat bathed him.

When their conga-line reached the edge of the river, Colin fell to his knees and submerged his head in the stream. He vacuumed up water until he ran out of breath. He resurfaced and took a long drag of fresh air. He wished the current were weaker so he could wade through the water, but, afraid of floating away, he simply cupped his hands and scooped. After pouring the water all over his body, cooling his burns, he drank a few more handfuls.

"Ready?" Rose asked.

"Almost." Colin didn't look up. He pulled out a couple of beets from the cuff of his pants. He alternated between biting a beet and slurping some water. After he finished, he turned around and saw Emma wobbling away.

Rose handed Colin her tail. Together, they limbo danced after Emma, ducking under invisible poles.

"How far are we from the House of Rex?" Emma asked after they caught up to her.

"Halfway," Rose said.

"Only halfway?" Emma sped up her wobble.

"Almost halfway. And no need to rush, we'll be there by morning."

"Promise?" Emma restlessly relaxed.

Rose nodded, her head upside-down as she continued her limbo. "When we reach the bend," Rose pulled her tail out of Colin's hand to point it out, and only then did he see the bend before them, "we will come to the end of the river, to Parrot's Point."

Colin wondered what she meant by Parrot's Point. Besides the Discodactyls, he hadn't seen a single bird in the Days of the Dinosaur. But he didn't ask about the possibility of discovering parrots, he figured he'd find the answer soon enough. He decided to reach for the dinosaur's tail again, and he daydreamed as they embraced. He shut his eyes as he danced with her, and he imagined Rose wrapping her tail around his limbo stick, dragging him along as he ducked beneath the parade of plummeting bars. Before his fantasy could come to completion, they danced around the bend and came to the lagoon, and the jeering of the Sex Pistols' "Friggin' in the Riggin'" sailed through the salty air.

Rose steered Colin into the forest, and Emma followed. "We can't let them see us," she said. "When we get to the last line of trees, I'll tell you how we'll get past them," she slowed down her limbo dance, "but for now the forest will protect us."

As they approached Parrot's Point, Colin first observed a pirate ship anchored in the center of the lagoon. It was an exact replica of the ship he had danced to the Days of the Dinosaur, except the figurehead looked more like a Triceratops than a Brontosaurus. He saw colorful bodies moving on the brig, but he couldn't discern any specific details from this distance. The water shined bright seaweed green. The sand burned dark burgundy. The river ran into the left side of the lagoon, and as they got closer, he realized another river ran down the right side of the shore. Past the sand and past the pirate ship, the lagoon simply ceased to exist, and behind the drop-off, the ocean stretched into eternity.

The bodies on the brig began to take shape. They had the same build as the Triceratops. The main difference about these dinosaurs, as far as Colin could tell, amounted to them wobbling when they danced. As he continued to diminish the distance between them, he saw that instead of having three horns on their heads, they hosted three tie-dye parrots. Over one eye they wore patches, and Colin finally saw why they wobbled: All the meat below their elbows and knees had been replaced by peg legs. Right as Colin realized this, he felt the sun smile down on him. Rose's neck wrapped around him and jerked him back into the forest.

"Not so fast," she said.

"Pirates," he said. "Prehistoric pirates!"

"Piratops," Rose said, uncoiling her neck from Colin.

He left his arm on her neck as she pulled away, and once she moved out of reach, it plopped against his side. "Piratops," he muttered, watching the pink and purple dinosaurs' as they danced.

One of the Piratops, the biggest of the bunch, sat on the poop deck. His or her skin had been polished a slick brown sheen, and

89

this dinosaur's backside hung over the rim. Below this beast, Piratops gathered in a mosh pit on the quarterdeck. For some time Colin tried to figure out why they fought. Then one of the Piratops finally seemed to get an advantage over the other prehistoric pirates, and without wasting a second, this dinosaur shoved his or her central parrot up the awaiting Piratops' anus. The Piratops hanging over the poop deck convulsed, and his or her parrots squawked. The dinosaur continued convulsing until one of the warring animals on the quarterdeck brought down the Piratops who had their parrot lodged deep inside the big one. Besides the moshing dinosaurs, other Piratops were spread sporadically along the main deck, some of them pulsated and some of them seemed to sift through sleep, their pink and purple skin stained a spectral blue.

"What are they doing?" Colin asked, refusing to remove his sight from the ship. "The ones fighting below the poop deck, I mean."

"King, or Queen, of the Poop Deck," Rose said, shaking her head. "It's a game they play, Bau knows why."

"How do they play?" Apparently, Emma hadn't been watching them war.

"The Piratops on the quarterdeck mosh until one of them gains some ground." As she spoke, one of the Piratops gained ground, as if Rose were narrating the events, despite not bothering to face the action. "When this dinosaur has secured some territory, he or she will shove their central parrot up the anus of the current King or Queen, sending convulsions throughout his or her Majesty's body."

Colin watched the pink and purple dinosaur mosh against the other Piratops, warring while parrot-deep in the Majesty's anus. The King or Queen continued to convulse, and Colin couldn't believe how well this quarterdeck Piratops had mastered multitasking.

"Once a Piratops has firmly inserted the central parrot into the Majesty's sphincter, the objective is to send convulsions throughout the Majesty until the King or Queen unloads the Royal Secretions." On cue, the Piratops sitting on the poop deck released a missile-sized shit onto the bodies of the moshing dinosaurs below. "When this feat is achieved, the champion, with his or her freshly secreted crown, wobbles up the ladder to the

90

poop deck, kicks the Majesty over the edge, and becomes the new King or Queen. Then the game resets and they do it all over again."

"That's the grossest fucking game I've ever heard of." Emma tried erasing what she'd just seen with her hands.

"It's pretty far out," Rose said.

"Look at the new Majesty," Colin said. "The old King or Queen is already parroting him or her." He watched the Majesty dump the Royal Secretions. "That Piratops is just too big. The fight's entirely unfair."

"To get to the House of Rex," Rose grabbed Colin with her tail and literally turned his attention toward her, "we have to dance across the shore to the river on the other side."

"Why don't we just groove through the forest?" Emma asked.

"Because its within the Arium of the Astralsaurus," Rose said, as if it were obvious. "Why else would we take the long way to the House of Rex?"

"The long way?" Emma asked.

"Yeah," Rose said, "the long way. The House of Rex is on the southwest corner of the island. We started at the northernmost point of the Days of the Dinosaur," she used her tail to trace their trek on an invisible map, "passed through the Astral of the Apatosaurus, which dropped us off on the southern side of the Northern Plains, before heading east to the Big River. We followed that down here, to the southeast edge of the island, to Parrot's Point."

"We took the fucking long way?" Emma huffed. "If we had taken the short way, would we be with Joe by now?"

"Hypothetically," Rose said. "Assuming we made it through the Arium of the Astralsaurus safely, yes, I dare say we would."

"Fucking cunt!" Emma lunged at Rose. Colin bunny-hopped between them and caught Emma, using her momentum to propel them into a tango. Shouting over his shoulder, she said, "We haven't saved Joe yet because you didn't want to see some dinosaurs? There're dinosaurs all over this fucking island. It's the fucking Days of the Dinosaur."

In the throes of their tango, Colin grabbed a stick of celery from his shirt and slapped it across Emma's face before biting into the vegetable. "Calm down, Emma," he said with his mouth full, "I'm sure Rose has her reasons, right?" The celery slap seemed to bring Emma's rage down a notch. He let go of her and sat down, tired from his heated tango. "So Rose, why did you guide us along the long road to the House of Rex?"

"If we went through the Arium of the Astralsaurus, we'd have absolutely no shot at survival. If we make it through Parrot's Point, we'll be pushing our luck as it is, dancing through the River of Rex, which is surrounded by the Arium of the Astralsaurus on both sides. It's a long shot, but it's the only path offering the possibility of passage."

"Fine," Emma said, seething. "So how do we get through Parrot's Point?"

"Easy, like I said earlier, all we have to do is headbang across the shore."

"Where anyone can see us?" Emma exclaimed.

"Not just anyone," Rose said, "only the Piratops."

"As we came around the bend, didn't you say we should dance through the forest to avoid being seen by the Piratops?" Emma practically shouted. Colin hoped the pirate ship's constant repetition of "Friggin' in the Riggin'" had hardened the Piratops' hearing. "Aren't they the reason we're hiding here now?"

"Yes," Rose said, "quite right. But up until now, the Piratops have been our sole threat. So dancing in the open would have been a futile risk. Once we cross the Big River though, we'll be in the Arium of the Astralsaurus. And given our options, headbanging along the shore before the Piratops will be significantly safer than potentially crossing paths with an Astralsaurus. Trust me, it's best to keep that option off the dance-floor as long as possible."

"So headbanging through the sand is the plan," Emma said. "What could go wrong?"

"If Rose says we'll be fine, we have nothing to worry about." Colin nodded. He thought the nod might add extra encouragement.

"Piratops are notorious for not noticing things. Just look at them," Rose signaled the ship with her tail, "between playing King, or Queen, of the Poop Deck and reveling on the main deck, they won't see a thing."

"What did I tell you," Colin said.

Emma just rolled her eyes, shook her head.

"Last thing," Rose stretched her neck in preparation, "it's vital that you keep dancing toward the other side of the shore. Progress, your life may depend on it."

Rose headbanged past the last line of trees. Emma cut Colin off, headbanging behind Rose, and the Apatosaurus's tail slipped through his fingers. Discouraged, Colin headbanged behind them through the burgundy sand.

Colin kept his eyes on Rose as he danced across the first half of the shore. But once he hit the halfway mark, a pandemonium of parrots squawked. He stopped, turned to face the pirate ship, and headbanged in place. The biggest Piratops, who still occupied the poop deck, convulsed chaotically as three competitors on the quarterdeck had their central parrots crammed up his or her anus. All three of the dinosaurs on the quarterdeck moshed against each other, trying to edge one another out. As they warred, each of their two free parrots squawked uncontrollably, and the Majesty's convulsions increased astronomically. Long after the convulsions became impossible to count, the King or Queen's parrots shivered and shrieked, and the Majesty's Royal Secretions flooded the quarterdeck so that only the colorful heads of the Piratops' parrot-horns peeked out of the poop.

"What the actual fuck?" Colin said, barely above a whisper. But somehow, the Piratops must have heard him over the music, because the second the words left his lips, all the dinosaurs aboard the brig stopped what they were doing and turned toward him. "Shit," he searched for Rose and Emma, saw that they had just reached the River of Rex. "Double shit!"

"Colin!" Rose screamed, simultaneously banging her head and tail against the sand, causing the shore to quake as if she were trying to shake his legs out of their paralysis. Still, he wouldn't budge, unable to bring himself to headbang closer to his dream dinosaur. Beside the Apatosaurus, Emma hopped up and down, waving her hands frantically above her head.

All the Piratops moshed over the edge of the pirate ship, diving into the lagoon. "Rose!" Colin cried. "Emma! Help!" He couldn't stop staring at the sea. He scanned the surface for signs of life, but the lagoon had fallen eerily quiet. As he stood there in silence, he felt spiders crawl across his skin, excreting sticky stems of silk. No matter how much he slapped and scratched, he couldn't alleviate the feeling of being crawled upon.

Suddenly, a passel of Piratops shot out of the lagoon, moshing across the burgundy shore. Colin shoved a couple of fingers into his mouth and chewed on the nails until he could taste blood. He watched the dinosaurs stumble through the sand on their peg legs. The sun glinted off the parrots protruding from their heads, and he realized the birds had evolved into feathered sabers. The Piratops swooped their sabers through the air as they danced closer and closer to Colin. Petrified by the Piratops, Colin continued to headbang in place.

Besides slamming his head up and down, up and down, he didn't move until the Piratops were within Apatosaurus tail-twisting distance. And even then, he didn't really move; he flinched. He dug his heels into the sand, squatted, and shielded his banging head with his hands. Colin closed his eyes.

He heard the contact of bodies colliding with each other, but he didn't feel it. He saw his life flash before his eyes, and he assumed that the sensation of being speared by a series of sabers must take some time. But after a few minutes passed painlessly, Colin opened his right eye and lowered his fleshy shields. Once he glimpsed an army of unconscious Piratops before him, he leapt, punching the sky with his fist, headbanging hedonistically. When his feet landed in the sand, he watched Rose and Emma windmill through the last line of Piratops as they retreated toward their ship. Amazed, Colin marveled that the Apatosaurus of his dreams could breakdance. She spun on the ground from her back to her belly, using her tail and neck to lift her whenever she passed over her stomach, keeping her feet off the ground. And when she rolled over her back, she bashed in the brains of the Piratops with her pillaresque legs. After Rose and Emma knocked out every Piratops on the shore, they headbanged over to Colin.

"Awesome," Colin said.

"Are you okay?" Rose pressed her tail into his hand.

"What the fuck, Colin? Rose said to keep moving no matter what. You could've ruined everything!"

"I know, and I'm sorry." He squeezed Rose's tail. "Thanks for coming back! I thought I was dead for sure."

Emma breathed deeply. "Like what else could we have done?" She sounded annoyed. "Rose and I wouldn't last an hour together. Without you in the middle, we'd never make it to Joe."

94

"I don't know," Colin said, smiling, "but you two do make a pretty incredible crew."

"Let's keep moving," said Rose, ignoring Colin's comment. She stepped back on the balls of her feet, swiveled her heels outward, and shaking her body, she danced backward toward the River of Rex. "We still have a lot of ground to cover before the sun sets."

Colin and Emma followed Rose's lead, mirroring her mashed potato as they entered the Arium of the Astralsaurus, leaving behind the Battle of Burgundy Beach.

Post-Summer Sickness (Chapter Eighteen)

COLIN THOUGHT HIS BROTHER WAS GOING TO DIE. He and his friends had been back in school for about a week and a half when Joe became ill. They had just started their third year of college, and Joe and Emma had just spent their first summer in Seattle together. Joe had stayed healthy over the break, and consequently, this had been his first time getting sick after his splenectomy.

Joe had woken up with a head cold, and he and Emma decided to ditch class to prevent his illness from growing. By the time Colin had returned to their campus apartment at the end of his day, Joe's cold had morphed into the flu. When Colin entered their unit, he turned left into the hall and headed toward his best friend's room.

"How's he doing?" Colin asked, shouting down the corridor.

"I called the doctor and they said he'd need to go to the hospital if he gets any worse," Emma shouted back.

As Colin reached the doorway, Emma replaced the pot beneath her boyfriend's string of vomit. Joe lay hunched over the side of his bed, puking repeatedly into a variety of pots. Five pots were already full, and Joe now worked on filling the sixth.

"Hey Colin," Joe murmured, waving absentmindedly between heaves.

Colin nodded, disgusted by the number of filled pots. He

wondered how someone could contain so much vomit. It reminded him of last semester when he got alcohol poisoning during the dance team's spring break party.

"Will you dump some of this shit down the toilet?" Emma asked, replacing the sixth pot with a seventh. "We're almost out of pots."

"Yeah, sure," Colin said, grabbing a pot to carry to the bathroom. "Don't use the last clean one, though. I'm going to make some soup."

"Just hurry," Emma said, "before this one fills, too."

Colin dumped four of the pots in the toilet before he brought the clean one to the kitchen and started heating up some canned soup. As he waited for the broth to boil, and Joe continued to heave down the hall, Colin thought this must have been what the doctors meant by him getting any worse. Joe had filled almost a dozen pots to the brim with vomit by now, and he didn't show any signs of slowing. His body had to have been nearly depleted of its liquid. Colin stirred the soup, wishing it would boil already. His brother needed it. Joe hated dry heaving more than anything in the world, or at least that's what he had said a couple of weekends ago as he knelt before their toilet after the dance team's back-to-school party.

The soup finally started to bubble. Colin turned off the stovetop and poured two bowls, one for Joe and one for Emma. He carried them to his brother's room, but the instant he saw Joe, the bowls crashed against the carpet and cracked.

"We need to go to the hospital," Colin said, staring at the blood drooling into the pot from Joe's colorless lips.

Emma just nodded.

"I'll bring my car around front," Colin said, already heading for the door.

He sprinted down the stairs of their apartment complex. In the underground parking garage, he ran to his pterodactyl-themed VW Bus. His car coughed to life, and as he left the lot, Strawberry Alarm Clock's "Incense and Peppermints" sounded from the stereo.

Astralsaurus Showdown (Chapter Nineteen)

"**You know she's just using you,**" Emma said, gesturing to Rose, who danced up ahead. Earlier, the Apatosaurus decided to inspect the forest for Astralsauruses, to guarantee them the safest possible passage.

Colin faced Emma in disbelief as they did a simultaneous Charleston up the River of Rex. "What do you mean?"

"Ever since I saw them doing the Apatosaurus Quadrille, I knew something wasn't right. Their dance was fucking fantastic. We never should have won."

"But they said they'd never seen anyone dance like us. We won because we brought something new to their world."

"Exactly, they were lying. Do you honestly believe there's a single dance they haven't seen before? Have you not realized Rose, and all the other dinosaurs, know every dance known to humankind?"

"Then how do you explain Rose asking me to teach her to salsa?" Colin sounded triumphant.

"She was acting. She was better than you from the first step."

"I'll admit they're incredibly dance-literate," Colin said, deflated. "But that doesn't prove anything."

"How do you think they learned all these dances? We aren't the first future dancers to come to the Days of the Dinosaur. People have probably been dancing pirate ships back here for ages."

"Just because dancers from the future came here before us doesn't mean the dinosaurs know everything about dance. What if we're the first modern dancers, and our style of dance is what they've been yearning for all this time?"

"Think back to the cave paintings in the Astral of the Apatosaurus."

"What about them?"

"The humans in the paintings were dancing Gangnam Style, which means they couldn't have come more than a few years before us."

"Bullcrap, you're screwing with me."

"It was shitty, even hard to recognize, but after some serious pondering, I'm positive."

"Okay," Colin said, still doubtful the cave paintings did in fact depict people doing Gangnam Style, "so let's pretend you're right, they know every dance ever. That doesn't mean any of the previous dancers were as talented as you and Joe."

"Maybe if Joe and I were dancing, we could have been the best they've ever seen. But we weren't. It was me and you and we were shit. But I don't think it matters who the challengers were. Even someone as good as your mom would've lost with objective judges."

"Now I know you're messing with me."

"I'm serious. They know every dance in history. Not only that, despite their size, they've overcome gravity to master dance. There's no way any futuristic dancers could do better in a dance-off against the Tyrannosaurus Rex than the Apatosauruses."

"Then why go through all this trouble? Why wait for futuristic dancers and why give us their prophecy? Why didn't they just send their best to defeat the Tyrannosaurus Rex decades ago?"

"I wasn't sure until we saw the Tyrannosaurus Task Force. Remember when I asked Rose why we were hiding and she said it was to keep the Tyrannosaurus Rex from knowing about their species' existence?"

"Yeah," Colin said, his Charleston now just a series of continuous knee-bumps.

"I think they haven't sent their best to challenge the Tyrannosaurus Rex because they're afraid of losing, of revealing their existence. As to the prophecy, they probably just made that shit up."

"It has to be real. How else would they have gotten their Astral? How would they know futuristic dancers were coming?"

"I don't know," Emma said, her Charleston now a series of knee-bumps, too, "but their Astral was only ever meant to be a temporary safe haven. I think they got scared of being discovered, and instead of risking it, decided to wait for futuristic dancers to take care of their problems for them."

"Even if it were somehow true, this still doesn't explain Rose's attraction to me, why she's so intent on keeping me safe and by her side."

"Nothing explains that," Emma said, smiling, "but seriously, Rose and I would never make it to the House of Rex without you. Rose is leading you on in order to get us to do what she wants: Challenge the Tyrannosaurus Rex in the Ultimate Dinosaur Dance-Off. I bet once we arrive on the outskirts of the House of Rex, she'll ditch us. And if we don't beat the Tyrannosaurus Rex for them, Rose will move on and wait for the next potential savior to sail through time."

"Colin, Emma," Rose said, as she hula-danced toward them. "There's a cloud of Astralsauruses ahead. Avoid direct eye contact."

Colin wanted to refute Emma's attacks on Rose's reputation, but the dinosaur now danced within hearing distance. Besides, no matter how much it pained him to admit it, something about Emma's words felt axiomatic. And as Rose rejoined her friends, she slid her tail into his hands.

The dinosaur's tail trembled, causing Colin to shake. He forced a smile, but when she smiled back, his worries withered. And as Froth's "Oaxaca" began to seep from the trees, floating eyes blinked throughout the bushes.

"Keep your eyes on me," Rose said, facing her friends, hula dancing backwards through the Arium of the Astralsaurus.

Colin nodded as his hips swayed from side to side. He stretched his left arm above his head and bent his other elbow so his right arm hung at his chest, both hands shaking. Beside him, Emma mirrored his movements.

—

Colin sensed the eyes of the Astralsauruses following him, heard them when they blinked. He felt slightly violated and endangered. Mostly, though, he felt jealous. He wished he could watch them like they watched him. No human had discovered this dinosaur's fossil, but if he could only find the courage to look away from Rose, he would see them in their natural habitat. He thought of the Piratops and the Discodactyls, and his desire to see an Astralsaurus surged.

"We're almost out of the cloud," Rose said, restless. "Just half a mushroom dance-floor more."

What could possibly be so dangerous about glimpsing an Astralsaurus? They were already being watched, so why not return the gesture? Colin kept his eyes on Rose, but every time she blinked or glanced at Emma, the idea of missing this opportunity to spot an Astralsaurus became borderline unbearable. Colin tried focusing on his moves, but since his hula never broke out of its basic structure, the only variation of the dance being when he switched the positions of his arms, it failed to keep his attention for more than a few seconds. His mind kept wandering back to the Astralsauruses. Since Rose thought they were so dangerous, they were probably some kind of carnivore. But were they raptors or tyrannosaurs or something else entirely? Were they big or small? And what about them specifically were they trying to avoid?

"Just a few more sways," Rose said, still hula dancing backwards.

And what if Emma were right? What if Rose had been using him to free her species from the Tyrannosaurus Rex? After all, during their dance-off against the Apatosauruses, she had twisted her tail with another dinosaur rather romantically. Maybe she loved that Apatosaurus, and each time she had placed her tail in Colin's hands, it had meant nothing to her.

His last chance to see an Astralsaurus had practically passed. A few steps ahead, Rose paused her progress and shook her hips in place. Colin heard her sigh over Froth's song, and she smiled at him before eyeing Emma. When Rose broke their connection, Colin chanced a glance back at the Astralsauruses. All he could see were their eyes, hundreds of them, blinking throughout the trees on both sides of the river. The eyes had no bodies. Floating in the air, they bobbed up and down.

A pair of eyes looked at Colin as he started to turn back to Rose. They blinked, and although he knew he had kept turning his head, that he now looked at the Apatosaurus again, the image of the blinking eyes before the forest had consumed his vision, as if his visual perception were frozen in time. Clouds of mist started to crawl into the picture, seeping out of the Astralsaurus's eyes, spreading a minty scent. The mist grew too thick to see into, and as it slowly approached, the music's volume increased, cancelling all other sound. He screamed Rose's name, reached for her tail, but nothing happened.

The mist clouds continued to creep toward Colin, but everything else remained stagnant. Seconds felt like centuries as he waited to be enveloped, and when Froth's "Oaxaca" prepared to climax, the clouds finally came, conquering his visual stagnation. His vision shot toward Rose, and as it caught up to the present, he heard himself shouting her name, saw his arm reaching for her tail, while gravity pulled him and Emma away from the Apatosaurus. The mist now encircled them, as if they were inside a hollowed-out pipe made of clouds. The cloud clearing kept carrying Rose further and further from them, only stopping once it had stretched twenty Apatosauruses long. The pairs of floating eyes peeked out of the cloud walls, just like they had with the trees. But as the eyes came closer, bodies began to emerge from the mist.

The Astralsauruses stood roughly five-feet tall. They sported toothy, blue beaks and red-feathered coats. Their arms were winged and ended in modest, blue claws. Their talons probably allowed them to climb trees, which would explain why some of the floating eyes were higher than others. Their legs were muscular and lean, and they two-stepped on massive curved claws. Their tails were roughly as long as their bodies, and in their entirety they stretched about ten feet. They resembled colorful Deinonychuses, the much larger and more dangerous relative of the Velociraptor. They stepped back into the coverage of the clouds, and Colin wished he had never risked looking at the Astralsauruses. He shivered.

"Rose," Emma shouted, "what's happening?"

"One of you must have made direct eye contact. They've taken us to their world, to the Astral Plane. Now you're separated from the thing you want most, and you have to dance your way through an army of Astralsauruses to reach it!"

"But you're at the other end," Emma said, doing a stationary hula. "Shouldn't I be seeing Joe?"

"Were you the one who looked into their eyes?"

"Goddamnit, Colin." Emma glared at him. "First the Piratops and now this?"

"I'm sorry," he said, "I couldn't help it."

"Bullshit! What if we don't make it to the other side? What if Joe dies because you can't control your fucking eyes?"

Colin stayed silent. From the other side of the clearing, Rose smiled at him, sadly shaking her head. He blushed. Not only did discovering a living Astralsaurus put them in this situation, it also inadvertently informed Rose that he wanted her more than anything in the world.

"So all we have to do is dance to you," Emma shouted, "and then we can get back to rescuing Joe?"

"Yeah," Rose said, "but be careful. I've never seen an Astralsaurus on its Plane before. I have no idea what they're capable of."

"After you," Emma said to Colin. "You got us into this shit, now you're going to get us out."

"But what dance should I do?"

"I don't fucking care. A shuffle? A slowfox? A fucking fandango?"

"Okay," Colin said, "clap."

"I was joking," Emma said.

"Stomp your feet and clap."

"I fucking hate the fandango."

"Just clap," Colin tapped his feet in place, smiled suavely, "and I'll show you how it's done."

Emma rolled her eyes and clapped along to the song and Colin's tapping feet.

"Rose," Colin shouted, placing one hand on his hip and sweeping the other before him, gesturing to the clearing, "clap to the beat of my feet!"

The Apatosaurus smacked her head against her body, synchronizing her sounds with the dance.

Colin stepped forward, transitioning from his left foot to his right, which tapped as it touched the ground. As he prepared to spin around, he angled his left foot like a hockey stick and

103

brought it back down. But before his big toe landed, an Astralsaurus torpedoed out of the cloud wall, colliding with Colin's back. They crashed against the white floor, and by the time Colin understood what had happened, an Astralsaurus pile had already buried him.

"I was wrong," Colin's voice bled through the dinosaurs' bodies, "forget the fandango. Help!"

He felt like he'd been steamrolled as the Astralsauruses' claws stabbed and cleaved at his skin. Colin strained for air. But before he lost it completely, the Astralsauruses were kicked off his body.

Colin stood up, felt faint, and fought it with deep breaths and a two-step. Once the dizziness passed, he saw Emma lying just above the ground, using her right hand to spin herself in circles and her feet to kick away Astralsauruses. He danced in the wake of her jackhammer, jumping into the air and spinning in a circle with his arms extended and his feet together. Colin's continuous *tours en l'air* took care of any lingering Astralsauruses. After Emma knocked them down, his slapping hands kept them from getting back up.

Colin grew incredibly dizzy as he repeatedly spun through the air. His vision blurred and he couldn't tell which Astralsauruses were raising and which were falling. Worse, he couldn't even differentiate between the dinosaurs and the cloud walls. He could only see a coalescence of color, and every couple of turns his hands would slap feathery flesh. At one point, Emma burst into hysteric screams, but after four or five rotations these transformed into rhythmic groans. Colin spun and spun. He vomited in the middle of a rotation, and spun some more. He started to worry that his perpetual *tours en l'air* might make this dizziness permanent. But ten or twenty spins later, he danced into a solid wall and crumpled to the floor. He vomited again as the world around him continued to tornado.

Suddenly, gravity yanked Colin down, and while the spinning persisted, he plunged through the cloud floor. Even though his body had been glued to the ground, he felt like the Earth had suctioned him into its core, causing him to crash through layer after layer. Falling through the Earth didn't hurt. It felt like being crushed under a wave, intense and terrifying, but practically painless. Colin vomited once more before the dizziness started to dwindle. And once it had finally passed, and he saw the grass he lay on, the gravitational force started to subside.

The nausea dissipated slowly. Colin became aware of his surroundings in incremental steps. He lay beside the River of Rex, and the Arium of the Astralsaurus surrounded him on both sides. Trees waved in the wind, and the cloud of Astralsauruses had fled.

"Rose!" Colin called, sitting up, "Emma!"

"Colin," Rose faced away from him, and speaking to the distance, she said, "come here."

Colin stood and stretched.

"Now!"

Colin jumped and quickly two-stepped over to Rose, who sat twenty feet up the river. Before he reached her side, he asked, "What's wrong?"

Rose didn't bother answering. Colin two-stepped beside her. She had her neck coiled around Emma like a Slinky.

"Stop," Colin said, "what're you doing?"

Rose's words were muffled, as if she had been speaking without moving her mouth.

"What?"

Rose loosened her grip on Emma, and blood drooled from the left side of her body. "Your shirt," she said, and squeezed once more.

Colin looked at his shirt. There were a few holes clawed out of it from his time spent at the bottom of the Astralsaurus pile. Thankfully, they failed to breach the last few layers of vegetables. "What about my shirt?"

Rose relaxed her neck and shouted, "Give it to me."

Colin lifted his shirt over his head, and a variety of vegetables fell to the floor. Bending over, he handed the shirt to Rose, and she grabbed it gently between her teeth.

"What's wrong?" he asked.

Rose uncoiled her neck. A dull white knob poked its head through the red where Emma's left hand used to be.

"Shit," Emma screamed as her blood flowed freely.

Colin grew light-headed. "Rose, is there any calamite around? Anything I can do?"

"I don't know." Rose attempted to tourniquet the wound with Colin's shirt. She used her tail to hold one end in place, and she wrapped the other end around Emma's arm again and again with her mouth. After the arm had been thoroughly wrapped, Rose attempted to tie a knot. She struggled tightening it. On the final tug, the shirt kept slipping through her teeth. Gargling blood, she said, "Pull this," and motioned to the end of the shirt with her eyes.

Colin pulled as hard as he could, accidentally jerking Emma's arm in the process, and she moaned. Once he had tied it taut, he let go of the shirt and wiped the blood off on the grass. When he had finished, Rose moved her tail toward his hands. Even though it would smear Emma's blood all over him again, he squeezed her tail three times. Despite the unnecessary danger he put them in and despite his unintentional declaration, she still wanted him to hold her tail. Maybe Emma had misjudged Rose's intentions. As he held her tail he thought, maybe this could be love.

"The tourniquet's as good as it'll get," Rose said. "You're still bleeding, but now it's manageable."

Emma nodded. She'd been nodding since Rose started speaking. Her face had turned pale and her eyes had bags.

"Emma, do you hear me?"

"Yeah," she said.

"Good." Rose continued, "Colin and I are going to search for some calamite. We'll be back soon. Just stay put and conserve all the energy you can."

"I'm going with you," Emma said, sitting up.

"For the love of Bau," Rose said, "You just lost your hand, not to mention all the blood. You need to rest."

"And Joe's going to lose his life if we don't keep moving. I'll rest when I'm dead, but till then, I'm going to save Joe." Emma stood and started to shimmy up the River of Rex, but before she made it ten steps she started to falter.

"You need to rest," Colin said. "You can't even dance straight."

"If you're going to find calamite," Emma said, wobbling, "it'll be on the way to the House of Rex. I'm going." Emma shimmied another twenty or thirty feet before tipping over. She lifted herself back up, danced a few more feet, and collapsed.

Rose stood and awkwardly two-stepped toward her. It only took her a few steps to reach Emma's side. "You're right," she said, bending her neck. "You're coming, but you aren't dancing. I'm going to carry you."

Colin had now risen and skipped toward them. Rose had lightly clamped her teeth around Emma's remaining hand and gently lifted her onto her back.

"Thanks," Emma said.

"Don't mention it." Rose smiled. "But we'll only go on one condition."

"What's that?" Emma frowned.

"We're a couple hours from the House of Rex." Colin caught up to Rose as she spoke. "We'll reach it around sunset. And when we do, we sleep through the night. Only once we're rested will we come up with our plan to save Joe."

"Fine," Emma said.

Rose slid her tail into Colin's left hand. Following her lead, he hand-jived toward the House of Rex, using his free hand to clap against his body to the rhythm of The Jimi Hendrix Experience's "Crosstown Traffic." As Rose smacked her head against her hips, Emma rested on her back, apparently unconscious.

Fraser River (Chapter Twenty)

Sunbeams reflected off the snowy mountaintop onto the turquoise water below. Across Berg Lake, which lies at the base of Mount Robson's north face, spruce and fir trees towered. Colin thought of Christmas as he lay in the cool spring soil before lazily turning away from the trees toward the lake. The turquoise water started to glow, and as the small boombox beside him played The Beatles' "Lucy in the Sky with Diamonds," the lake's surface rainbowed.

Joe and Emma were off in the forest somewhere, getting freaky, Colin suspected. All three of them had hiked the twelve miles from the Robson Meadows Campground to the lake. But apparently thirty minutes had been enough time for Joe and Emma to appreciate the place they had hiked five hours to see. Now an hour had passed since they became bored, or horny, and had ditched him. Alone, Colin had turned on the boombox, snuggled down into the soil, and spaced out. As the hits kept coming, the beauty of British Colombia had enveloped him.

Halfway between Colin and Mount Robson, Berg Lake's rainbow-colored water began to bubble. Slowly, a Triceratops-sized kokanee broke through the freshwater surface. Once the fish perched itself atop the lake, it tipped forward, dipping its green head underwater. With its head submerged, the fish's vibrant red body became completely vertical. Holding its aquatic handstand, the kokanee began to flop its body toward the forest as if it were signaling for Colin to turn around. He let the fish flop for a couple more minutes, but as The Beatles' song concluded, and the animals were immersed in the short silence between tracks, Colin rolled over. As Cream's "Sunshine of Your Love" blared from the boombox, a group of trees morphed together, forming the body of an Apatosaurus.

Colin suddenly shot up to his feet and flicked his head to the right, flinging his brown hair out of his eyes. He walked toward the tree cluster, consciously moving in slow motion. The Apatosaurus winked at him as he approached, and he nodded to the trees as if he were the king of cool. They opened their collective arms, and as the song entered its initial chorus, Colin and the wooden dinosaur embraced.

He climbed up the Apatosaurus's body, and when he reached her mouth, he leaned in and planted a sloppy kiss on her lips. After a minute, the dinosaur told him to lick her skin, and he obliged. He climbed across the Apatosaurus and licked her all over. Right after Cream's climax, Colin heard the sound of someone coughing, but he ignored it and continued to lick and suck the dinosaur. However, when the song came to a close, and the coughing persisted, Colin glanced up from the Apatosaurus. From the corner of his eye, he saw Joe and Emma standing before him, and the lake glowed from behind the two.

"What the hell are you doing?" Emma asked, confused. As she spoke, The Cyrkle's "Red Rubber Ball" came from the boombox.

The Apatosaurus he hugged returned to its original form, and Colin pulled a tree branch out of his mouth. "Nothing," he said, a little too loud. "What're you doing?" Each time he spoke, his tongue and gums prickled with pain, and the taste of aluminum flooded his mouth.

"We're going back to the campground," Joe said, looking past his twin brother. "It'll be dark in a few hours, and we're hoping to make it back before then."

Colin climbed down from the tree and joined Joe and Emma. As he picked up his boombox, he asked them how their walk went, but they gave him the silent treatment. His tongue felt like a porcupine.

"What were you doing to that poor tree?" Emma asked. She sounded as if she had been personally assaulted. She had a soft spot for plants.

Colin blushed but didn't say anything. Ever since he had stopped kissing the tree, the pain had intensified continually, and now his mouth hurt too much to talk. He started picking splinters off his tongue.

And as he followed Joe and Emma back through Berg Lake Trail, hiking toward their campsite along the Fraser River, "Red Rubber Ball" reverberated throughout Mount Robson Provincial Park.

Love in the Days of the Dinosaur (Chapter Twenty-One)

"I'M SO SICK OF DANCING," Colin said, unable to catch his breath. He held Rose's head in his left hand and her tail in his right as he led her in a sloppy oberek. They stepped three times to the left and three to the right, and they repeated this process again and again as they spun quickly up the River of Rex to the Grateful Dead's "The Golden Road (To Unlimited Devotion)."

"You're sick of dancing? I've been dancing ever since I was hatched."

"You're used to it."

"I've been dancing with all this extra weight." She motioned to Emma, who still lay on her back, unconscious.

"Now you're just fishing. She's light as a leaf to you."

Rose curved her colorful lips and flashed her spatulate teeth. "Don't worry, we're almost there. Once we reach the top of this hill we should be able to see the House of Rex."

"Awesome," Colin said, and he held Rose's appendages a little tighter. Until this point, the slope's incline had been moderate, but as they neared the top of the hill, it became nearly vertical. The stream had transformed into the base of a waterfall, and the grass path grew steps. They were roughly two mushroom dance-floors away from the top of the hill. "Can I ask you a personal question?"

"Surely," she said.

Colin had been wrestling with the wording of this question ever since they started their ascension, and he still hadn't gotten it quite right. Afraid the perfect combination of sounds might not exist, and convinced that he'd never find them even if they did, he blurted whichever words passed through his mind. "Was that longneck, I mean, Apatosaurus, who you twisted your tail with back home, your boyfriend?"

Rose burst into laughter. Colin's face flared tomato-red. "Never mind," he mouthed, and he led their oberek onto the first grass step. His right foot sank into it, and his left quickly followed. It reminded him of wading through the muddy, moss-covered bottom of a lake. He always hated the feeling of the moss and mud beneath his feet, between his toes, and their oberek suffered. Colin started leaping from his left to his right, and vice versa, instead of gently hopping. And he even occasionally stepped five or seven times to the same side, instead of three.

"I'm sorry," Rose said, "I shouldn't have laughed. But for what it's worth, no, he is not my boyfriend."

Colin audibly sighed with relief.

"Apatosauruses don't date," she said, "we mate."

"Oh," his face lost color, "so does that mean you're his mate?"

"Just for this season, thank Bau. He's so annoying."

"He is?" Colin said, hopeful.

"I can't stand him." Her face started to glow.

"Then why mate with him at all?" Maybe, if she disliked him so much, he could convince her to mate with someone else? Maybe she could mate with him?

"I admit, he certainly wasn't my first choice, but that's just how things matched up this season. Next year will be better. Any other mate would be better."

They were only a mushroom dance-floor away from the top of the hill, and despite Colin's attempts to prolong the length of their spins, he couldn't make the tempo of their oberek any slower than that of the Grateful Dead's song. "And you can't mate with anyone else?"

"No," she said, "not unless you find me another Apatosaurus with a fully functioning cloaca before the summer."

Colin's heart raced. He took a deep breath as they danced

together, their limbs intertwined. "Does it have to be an Apatosaurus?"

"It didn't used to," Rose said, "but now the only other dinosaurs out there are connected to the Tyrannosaurus Rex, and associating ourselves with associates of the Tyrannosaurus Rex is strictly forbidden."

"But," Colin said, his whole body perspiring, "do you have to mate with another dinosaur?"

Rose's glow grew, and a warm smile spread across her lips. She quickly killed it. "We only mate to reproduce. And I don't think we'd reproduce with anything except other dinosaurs."

Rose's smile, even if accidental, burrowed inside Colin's brain. He had a chance, an infinitesimal chance, but a chance all the same. "Do you ever mate because you want to?"

"Never," Rose said, her glow increasing. "Mating is nice, sure, but wouldn't you say making eggs for impractical reasons is a bit idealistic? Imagine if we chose our mates because they had the longest tail, or their color scheme was the brightest, or because they out-danced all the other dinosaurs, as opposed to being genetically compatible. Just think of how horrible our offspring could end up!"

"It can't be that bad."

"It is. Why do you think the Tyrannosaurus Rex wanted ultimate power?"

"I don't know."

"It's simple. It's because he mated with another Tyrannosaurus Rex for her feathers. She was the biggest Tyrannosaurus Rex in Prehistoric Paradise and she had such sensual, shiny golden feathers all over her body, and the soon-to-be tyrant didn't want anyone but her."

"There has to be more to it than that. How could desiring someone create a dictatorial dinosaur like the Tyrannosaurus Rex?"

"It's not technically his desire that created the problem, it was the inevitable next step: Consistency. Desiring the same dinosaur so strongly deadens the desire for other dinosaurs. And when a dinosaur desires only one dinosaur, DinoMania hatches."

"DinoMania?"

"DinoMania hatches when two dinosaurs decide to mate exclusively for long periods of time. It creates feelings of great excitement, euphoria, hyperactivity, and primarily, delusions. It's the most dangerous condition a dinosaur can inhabit."

"In what sense?"

"The Tyrannosaurus Rex wanted ultimate power because he wanted what was best for those whom he and his partner hatched. Their lives became infinitely more valuable than the lives of other dinosaurs. Therefore, when his golden-feathered love and their recently hatched offspring starved to death, he placed the blame on dinosaur society. He claimed that because they were carnivores, they needed meat to survive, and that the laws back then, which prohibited any dinosaur from eating another, were what killed his family. He was so enraged that he vowed revenge against every herbivore in existence. And shortly after that, the meteor caused the Earth to dance, and then the Tyrannosaurus Rex came with his genetically modified army, and together they enslaved every plant-eating species in the Days of the Dinosaur."

Colin felt entirely deflated. He had no idea how to get Rose to fall in love with him, or if it were even possible for her to love singularly. Sure, she liked him, her accidental smile showed that. But did she like, like him? Hopelessly, he asked, "And you don't think DinoMania is possible when you only mate temporarily and for genetic purposes?"

"Of course not. Look at the Astral of the Apatosaurus. Each dinosaur has numerous offspring with numerous mates. Not only does having so many mates make us less protective of them, which helps us treat all dinosaurs equally, it's also nearly impossible to meet another Apatosaurus who hasn't shared a mate, or at least shared a mate of a mate. And when someone you care about cares about someone, you're more likely to care for them, too."

It took Colin a minute to grasp Rose's sentiment.

"And when you care for your cared one's cared one," she continued, "it's hard to become DinoManic."

"Right..." Colin said, thoroughly unsure.

"Before the Tyrannosaurus Rex came to power, all sorts of dinosaurs mated with each other. Prehistoric Paradise only collapsed when the Tyrannosaurus Rex became DinoManic and decided to sidestep the system."

"But mating genetically just sounds so incredibly depressing,"

Colin pleaded, guiding their oberek onto the grassy plateau. "Is it worth it?"

"I don't know," Rose's face glowed again, a sudden burst of brightness. But her skin returned to its normal palette of constantly shifting green, purple, and blue tie-dye shades before she continued, "I admit, it's certainly not ideal, but it's our responsibility to dinosaurkind to mate with as many partners as possible. Because isn't risking a DinoManic society even more depressing?"

Colin shrugged, and as he spun Rose across the top of the hill, the House of Rex stretched into view.

Night (Chapter Twenty-Two)

ON THE OTHER SIDE OF THE PLATEAU, halfway to the sea below, a field of grass jutted out of the cliffside. In the center of the grass plane, the House of Rex stood twelve mega-Apatosauruses tall and its golden stipe stretched two mega-Apatosauruses long. Colin had never seen a mushroom bigger than the one before him. The stipe supported a chestnut brown cap streaked by cornflower blue smears. And although the surface of the cap remained flat, the stem constantly quaked, sending seismic ripples throughout the mushroom's roof and the Days of the Dinosaur. Beyond the House of Rex, the sea spanned infinitely, and Colin spied the rainbow sun as it sank below the horizon.

As Colin led Rose closer to the cliffside, he realized a waterfall separated them from the House of Rex. After the water crashed down onto the grass field, it circled the mushroom, creating a moat. The two torrents reunited on the other side before another waterfall spewed the liquid into the sea.

In the middle of the mushroom's cap, just above the stipe, the chestnut brown skin slid open. Slowly, the Tyrannosaurus Rex's boiling red head emerged from the hatch, nodding to OutKast's "Hey Ya!" as he stared at the sea. The dinosaur's horizontal body surfaced next. His torso resembled a golden, feathery walrus, and even his miniature winged arms shared some visual similarities with flippers. Swamp-green colored scales covered the dictator's lower body, starting with his hips and ending with the tip of his tail. The dinosaur reminded Colin of a gargantuan, half-shaved poodle. And then the legs appeared, long and lean.

Before the Tyrannosaurus Rex's entire body had risen out of the stipe, his only move consisted of a head nod. But once his clawed feet latched onto the wavy cap, and "Hey Ya!" progressed into its chorus, he lifted his short arms as high as he could, flapping them in rapid succession. Despite strenuously stretching until his limbs reached maximum height, his jazz wings only reached halfway up his back. He started to spin toward the plateau, but before Colin could catch a good glimpse of the Tyrannosaurus Rex's face, Rose twisted her neck around his body and hopped away from the cliffside as if her legs were pogo sticks.

Once they had passed the midpoint of the plateau, and the House of Rex had shaken out of sight, Rose hopped in place and uncoiled her neck. Colin sat and stretched. Motioning to the mushroom, he asked, "Did you know he was going to be like that?"

"Like what?" Rose's neck bounced each time she hopped, and she awkwardly wrapped it around Emma before lowering her to the ground. Despite her neck's constant jolts, she managed to gently set Emma down on the crystallized grass between Colin and the River of Rex.

"I don't know," he said, trying to answer her with his tone alone. "He just seemed so—pathetic."

"I was surprised," Rose admitted, "but I guess it doesn't matter how you look if you have an island of dinosaurs dancing under you." She leaned her head over the River of Rex. In its center, bubbles repeatedly burst. "We should wake Emma."

Colin nodded, and Rose filled her mouth with water.

The dinosaur rounded her lips, as if she were about to whistle, and shot a stream of water at Emma's face. Halfway through the second shower, Emma opened her eyes and brushed away the water. She didn't immediately react to a stump massaging her eye, her cheek, but before her face had dried, her eyes widened. She lifted her left arm, stretching the phantom limb before her, studying the stump. Colin thought about saying something encouraging, like that she'd still be able to perform plenty of dances outside of ballet break-dancing, but decided against it in case the ramifications of her fate still hadn't dawned.

Emma's panic slowly shifted to resignation, and as her glassy eyes stared at the starry sky, she said, "Why isn't it still bleeding?"

"There were some calamite trees along the base of the hill," Rose said. "They sealed the wound, but that's all they could do."

Emma stayed silent. Colin had seen her like this only once before, when she learned her parents and her beloved Bentley had been shot. That time, her resignation had lasted for a day, and it only stopped because Joe had asked her to move in with him, because he had insisted she'd always have a home with him for the rest of their lives. Colin had been useless then just like now. He wished Joe were here to fix this. He wished he could sneak into the massive mushroom to free his brother tonight.

"We all need sleep," Rose said. "Tomorrow we're going to face the Tyrannosaurus Rex."

Colin nodded as he lay down, and Emma remained unresponsive. Rose did the splits with both pairs of legs, resting on her stomach. She slipped her tail into Colin's hands. He brought it to his lips and kept it there until he fell asleep.

—

Colin felt something soft slink along his shin. He swatted it and rolled onto his side. The tail crept up his calf to the back of his thigh. He opened his eyes and saw the shadows of trees swaying in the moonlight.

"Colin," Rose whispered, "Colin, wake up."

Her tail now moved up his back. It moved over his side and rested against his chest. He hugged it, and she pulled him up. He wiped the crust out of his eyelashes as he sat in the dark. Rose lay on her stomach, sprawled out beside him, and her tail curved until it lay in his lap.

"I'm awake," Colin croaked, eyes still closed.

"Yeah?" Rose asked, amused.

"Yeah." Colin blinked his eyes open. "Is it time to rescue Joe?"

"Not yet," Rose said. "I couldn't sleep, and actually, I have a question for you."

"I'm listening." Colin suddenly felt jittery, as if he had drunk a couple of pitchers of coffee. The Animals' "We Gotta Get Out Of This Place" started to play softly overhead.

"Back home," Rose said, sounding almost tentative, "do you have a consistent mate? Like Emma has Joe?"

"No," Colin said, smiling, "not anymore."

"But you did in the past?" Rose asked, her voice sharp.

"Yes," Colin said, confused, "but I ended things a couple years before coming here."

The Apatosaurus nodded. Why did this matter? Could his relationship with Tracey somehow ruin whatever remaining chance he had of mating with Rose?

"Did you like it?"

"Yeah, kind of. It was complicated. Why?"

"No reason," Rose said, her face glowing in the darkness.

"Come on," Colin urged, "you can tell me."

"Okay," Rose said, anxiously. "I've always wondered what it'd be like to mate with another dinosaur consistently. Sometimes, I even wish an Apatosaurus loved me the way the original Tyrannosaurus Rex loved his mate. I mean, without the DinoMania, of course. And since you have mated consistently before, I was hoping to hear your thoughts."

"Oh," Colin said. His sunburn flared. "I'm probably not the best person to ask. My situation was a bit strange."

"What do you mean?"

"I mean, nothing was actually wrong with our relationship. I loved her, and she loved me. We could have been perfect together."

"Why weren't you?"

"I realized I was only into the idea," Colin said, sweat rolling from his chin to his chest, "and I finally accepted that I could never be truly happy unless I were with an Apatosaurus."

"Then why didn't you mate with an Apatosaurus?"

"Because," Colin said, unsure if Rose knew the fate of her species, "where I'm from, Apatosauruses don't exist anymore."

"But the prophecy," Rose protested, eyes wide, "says alien dancers from the future will save us from extinction by winning the Ultimate Dinosaur Dance-Off. And Reggie said you're the sign."

"Maybe we lose," Colin said. The second he heard the words aloud, the outcome felt absolute.

"The prophecy isn't wrong," Rose said.

"But what if we aren't right? We're not the first future dancers, and we probably won't be the last."

"You will be," Rose said, confident.

"How do you know?"

"Because, all the other dancers," she paused, and her glow grew, "all the other guides." She lifted her tail out of his hands and slowly dragged it along his skin. His pores became quivering bumps as her tail trailed up his stomach, his chest, his neck, before resting against his right cheek. He drowned in her amber scent. His whole body throbbed. "Because," she said, barely above a whisper, "I believe in you, Colin. Because I'm here for you, and together, we can defeat the Tyrannosaurus Rex."

Colin grabbed Rose's tail, pulled himself to his feet, and with outstretched arms, leapt as high as he could. He grabbed Rose's neck, just below her face, which, even when she lay down and curved it toward the ground, stood about eight feet above the crystallized grass. He wrapped his arms around her neck and raised his body until his feet hugged her, too, like a sloth hanging from a tie-dye branch. Colin tilted his head and looked into Rose's eyes. He leaned forward and kissed her colorful lips.

Colin couldn't believe it. Rose kissed him back. Did this mean she loved him? He'd been dreaming of this moment even since age nine, and now that the impossible had happened, he wished time would do him a favor and freeze.

Rose parted her lips slightly. Was this an invitation? Did she want part of him inside her? Slowly, he started to slide his tongue past his teeth, past his lips, until it brushed against the dinosaur's mouth. She parted her lips further, and he stretched his tongue as far as he could. It stopped between her teeth, which felt like enamel fingers, and his tongue swayed from side to side as if it were a toothbrush. Rose rubbed her tail along Colin's back, pressed his whole body tight against her neck as she rocked up and down.

Colin felt Rose's massive tongue tackle his. She tasted like lukewarm lettuce. He placed his hands on both sides of her snout, and as they continued to twist their tongues, continued to rub their bodies against each other, Colin thought he might come. But before he could, Rose jerked her neck, and Colin fell to the floor. He crashed against the crystallized grass.

"I'm sorry," Rose said, glowing.

"Don't be," Colin said, stretching out his arms, hoping to continue their embrace. "This is the best thing that's ever happened to me."

"Yeah, me too," Rose said, smiling weakly as she shook her head to the song. She started to dance away from Colin.

"Where are you going?"

"I'm sorry," Rose repeated, "but I'm starving. I haven't eaten anything all day, and there was a tree with tasty looking leaves halfway down the hill. I'll be back before dawn, I promise."

Colin tried to ask her what had just happened, what he had done wrong, but the further Rose danced into the distance, the louder The Animals' "We Gotta Get Out of This Place" blared. And by the time she had reached the edge of the plateau, The Animals had grown so boisterous that Colin became consumed—his entire universe contained in this song.

And then silence suddenly replaced it. Colin's ears rang as he scanned the land for Rose, but the dinosaur had disappeared.

The Breakup (Chapter Twenty-Three)

THE DINOSAUR PROPS weren't doing it anymore. It'd been almost a year and a half since he started dating Tracey, and he could hardly ever come. He still loved her. If he hadn't—he wished he didn't—breaking up with her would be easy. But the evolution of his love had turned entirely platonic. Simply put, Tracey's genetics kept her from transforming into a genuine Apatosaurus.

Colin first noticed his problem a year into their relationship, when Tracey went down on him while simultaneously stroking his chest with the head of a Utahraptor, the largest raptor to have ever lived. Even though Utahraptors were one of his favorite theropods, Colin couldn't finish. Over the next couple of weeks, the pterodactyls became useless, followed by the hadrosaurs, which were her favorite. Another month passed and the sauropod dinosaur props were the only ones to help. But even the sauropod stock depleted until Apatosauruses were the sole species that worked.

And the fact that Tracey had been the most perfect human partner he could have ever had made the whole situation even more tragic. She obsessed over dinosaurs, loved Colin's paleoart museum, and always preferred to use dinosaur props in bed. But no matter how hard he struggled to admit it, after sixteen and a half months, when even the Apatosauruses had stopped getting him off, he could no longer deny it. Colin had to end their relationship.

They had just finished finals and would be leaving campus the next day for winter break. They were in their second year, and Colin couldn't spend another couple of months, especially long-distance, pretending everything had been fine. They planned on meeting up at Dino's Diner for brunch before he left for the airport, and he figured he would break the news there.

The night before brunch she called him and invited him to stay the night. Not that this invitation had been unusual, they spent almost every night together. The question usually came down to whose dorm room they would sleep at. She sounded shocked when he said no.

"Why?" Tracey asked.

"Because I feel shitty," he said.

"Then I'll come to your place," she said, "I'll take care of you."

"No, don't," Colin said, "I don't want you to get sick."

"Okay." Tracey's tone clearly insinuated she knew Colin's claim reeked of bullshit.

"I'm sorry," he said, and he meant it. "I'll see you at Dino's."

"Yeah," she responded, and after a few seconds of silence, Colin hung up.

Colin arrived at Dino's Diner before Tracey, and he sat in *their* booth in the back. Tina, the waiter, stopped at his table and asked if he wanted the usual.

"Yes, please," Colin said. "Tracey's, too."

"Of course," Tina said. "I'll be right back with your Cokes."

"Thanks."

As she walked back to the kitchen, The 13th Floor Elevators' "You're Gonna Miss Me" played overhead, and he tapped his fingers along to the song as he waited. Tracey walked into the diner a few seconds after the song concluded. She spotted Colin at their table and smiled widely as she joined him, acting as if last night had never happened.

"Hey," she said, leaning over the table to give Colin a kiss before she sat down.

Colin kissed her back, smiled weakly, and held back tears. "Hi," he said, voicelessly. He cleared his throat and tried again. "Hey," he scratched his head, "I ordered your usual."

"Great," she said, as Tina delivered their sodas.

For the next couple of minutes, the only sounds came from the stereo as The Mamas and the Papas sang "California Dreamin'."

"Fitting," Tracey said, winking as best she could. "Are you excited to go back to San Fran?"

"I guess," Colin said, his hands fidgeting under the table. "You know, I've always loved it when you winked."

"Cause I look like an idiot?"

Indeed she did. She couldn't wink without pulling up half her mouth and wiggling her ear. "No," he said, "because you look adorable."

Tina delivered their food, saying, "One Tenontosaurus Melt for you," and she placed the tuna melt in front of Tracey, "and a Bambiraptor Burger for you. Enjoy."

Colin took a gigantic bite out of his venison burger. A minute later, after he'd finished chewing, he looked up. Tracey hadn't touched her Tenontosaurus Melt yet. Usually, she'd be halfway done already. "What's wrong?" he asked.

"Why are we doing this?"

Colin finished chewing the food in his mouth. He still didn't say anything.

"We both know what's wrong," she said.

"We do?"

"Goddamnit, do you need me to say it for you?"

"I'm so sorry, Tracey."

"I've known for a couple of weeks now. I'm not stupid, I just hoped it wasn't true."

"I still love you," Colin said, "I do. It's just..." he couldn't admit it. What if she hated him for it? What if even she didn't understand?

"I'm not an Apatosaurus?"

"Yeah," Colin's face brightened a bit, "how'd you know?"

"It's obvious," Tracey said, staying strong for another minute before breaking down. "And I know you love me," she wailed, "but you've also never loved me."

"I'm sorry." Colin started crying, too. He didn't know what else he could do.

They cried over their food for a few minutes. Then, through sniffles, they ate.

"I'm sorry," Tracey wiped her mouth with her hand, "it's just, I've tried so hard to be the dinosaur you want me to be, the dinosaur I want to be, but nothing I've done has made a difference. And it just sucks."

Colin nodded.

"But I want you to know that I still love you, and I'll always cherish our time pretending to be dinosaurs together, and I hope that you'll still love me in the ways you can."

"I do," Colin wiped his runny nose with a napkin, "I will."

Tracey stood and stepped toward Colin. But as he rose and opened his arms, she turned around and walked out of Dino's without looking back.

The Tyrannosaurus Rex v. Colin and Emma (Chapter Twenty-Four)

WHEN COLIN WOKE, the rainbow sun shined high in the sky and T. Rex's "Cosmic Dancer" roared. Mesmerized by the beauty of Marc Bolan's vocals, Colin rose to his feet and danced. Unaware of his surroundings, he shook his hips from side to side and waved his hands above his head. And as "Cosmic Dancer" climaxed, a flurry of feathery tails coiled around Colin's limbs, stiffening his dance into a stance. His reverie vanished, and he began to mosh.

He flailed his fists and stomped his feet, busting through a horde of Velociraptors. Once he broke free, he searched for Rose, but she had gone. Dozens of tails clasped his limbs, and Emma frantically shouted his name. She struggled against the Tyrannosaurus Task Force, but for every tail she escaped, five more clung to her. Colin no longer resisted. He didn't see the point. Rose hadn't returned, and Velociraptors had surrounded them from every angle. There were hundreds of them, possibly thousands, and they pushed his appendages together with their tails. They used twine to tie his arms above his head, to fasten his feet. And then, under the guidance of the Tyrannosaurus Task Force, he hopped toward the House of Rex.

The Velociraptors whipped them with their tails whenever they slowed their pace, which happened repeatedly before they made it to the edge of the plateau. Emma shouted, "I told you that dino-bitch would ditch us! And now, because you trusted her, Joe's going to die. We're all going to die." Colin just kept looking over his shoulder, scanning the opposite side of the cliff top, hoping to see Rose dance over the edge. She never appeared. And as the plateau disappeared, he stared at the House of Rex, blurred by the water pooling in his eyes.

As they hopped down the grass steps, Colin tried to avoid thinking of Rose. He listened to the noise of the waterfall crashing beside them, but it hardly created a sound over the powerful chords of "Cosmic Dancer." When they passed the last stair and started dancing across the grass plane toward the House of Rex, Colin pretended he and Emma were in a potato sack race and the first to reach the moat would win. He started to hop faster than the beat of the song, and the Velociraptors whipped him back into tune. As he continued his monotonous hop, his thoughts started to circle around Rose.

She had abandoned them. She had broken her promise. She didn't love him. But why had she kissed him back? Why did she ask him about his experiences with consistent mating? Why did she confide in him the way she wanted to be loved? It didn't matter. Nothing mattered. Emma had been right. Rose had ditched them despite the inevitable death her actions would bring them.

Tails wrapped around Colin and yanked him backwards, pulling him into the present. He hopped on the bank of the moat as the mushroom's drawbridge began its descent. He envisioned his head on the grass beneath the falling bridge. How bad would it hurt if it squashed his skull? He attempted to faceplant, but before his head reached the floor, resting beneath the drawbridge, multiple Velociraptor tails caught his body and forced him back to his feet. They whipped his naked back again and again. He wished he could crawl into the moat and have the current sling him around the House of Rex. The waterfall would swallow him and spit him into the sea.

Once the drawbridge had landed, the Velociraptors led him and Emma forward. Under the threat of their tail, Colin crossed the mushroom's threshold.

Inside the House of Rex, a long hallway had been hollowed out of the stipe. They passed various doors, each differing in size, but all sharing a gilled texture. About halfway through the stipe, the Tyrannosaurus Task Force veered left, and they hopped through the tallest doorway in the hall.

Colin and Emma were led into a courtroom. On the other end of the chamber, the Tyrannosaurus Rex sat behind the bench with a gavel between his teeth. The Velociraptors danced Colin and Emma to their seats at the defendants' table before heading over to the jury box. Once every creature had been seated, Iron Butterfly's "You Can't Win" reverberated throughout the courtroom.

The Tyrannosaurus Rex banged his head to the song, throwing down the gavel again and again. This lasted for almost a minute, but as the song slowed into its chorus, and the volume decreased dramatically, the judge dropped the mallet onto the bench and roared. The jurors shook. Emma glared ahead at the Tyrannosaurus Rex. Positive that the judge would eat them before declaring the verdict, Colin peed, drenching the vegetables that remained in his pants.

"Order! Order! Order!" The Tyrannosaurus Rex declared, his red head soaked in sweat. He picked up the gavel with his tail, banged it against the sound block, and looked directly at the defendants. "When you are found guilty, the charges brought against you, which include, but are not limited to: Roaming freely, lacking feathers or scales, being captured the morning before my dance-off, failing to enlist in my Task Force, and resisting arrest, are punishable by death, which will take the following form: Being live fed to the champion of the Ultimate Dinosaur Dance-Off at the celebratory feast. Once you are found guilty, the jurors," the Tyrannosaurus Rex pointed to the Velociraptors with his gavel, "will deliberate which of the accused will be served as an appetizer, and which of the accused will be served as dessert. What have you, defendants, to say for yourselves?"

"Is Joe alive?" Emma asked.

"Who?"

"Joe. Is he alive?"

"Objection, your honor," one of the Velociraptors interjected.

"Sustained," said the Tyrannosaurus Rex.

The juror who had objected hopped out of the jury box and danced up to the bench. The Velociraptor whispered something in the Tyrannosaurus Rex's ear and then hopped back to the box.

"Joe is alive," the judge said, "and his size is coming along nicely. Is that your only defense?"

"If I might add," Colin said, raising a finger in the air, "we would like to challenge you to the Ultimate Dinosaur Dance-Off."

The Tyrannosaurus Rex laughed. He asked, "And why would I do that?"

"Uh." Colin hadn't thought about it. He'd assumed the Tyrannosaurus Rex would accept the challenge. He suggested, "Because wouldn't you enjoy your feast even more if you knew you had just out-danced your meal?"

"Yes," said the Tyrannosaurus Rex, and he banged the gavel against the sound block. "And that is why two members of my Task Force were recently imprisoned for mutiny, and I'd rather defeat those traitors in my dance-off before savoring them as my personal dessert. Do the defendants," declared the judge, annoyed, "have any other defense?"

Colin looked at Emma helplessly. She started to respond, but before her words could formulate meaning, the Tyrannosaurus Rex interjected, "Very well." He banged his gavel. "The defendants have spoken." Addressing the Velociraptors, he said, "Did the jurors write all of that down?"

They didn't have anything to write on, never mind to write with, yet they nodded enthusiastically. They floated into the air as they smacked their tails together, and T. Rex's "Cosmic Dancer" overpowered Iron Butterfly.

"Order! Order! Order!" the judge shouted, smacking the sound block three times. The Velociraptors sunk to their seats and "Cosmic Dancer" died. As "You Can't Win" returned, the judge declared, "A verdict has been reached!"

Colin wondered why they went through the charade of having a trial. Clearly the outcome had been predetermined before they had even danced into the courtroom, and the jurors weren't even deliberating until after the sentencing. Not that it made any difference. He and Emma had failed Joe. His trust in Rose, his love for the Apatosaurus, would cause he and his brother and his friend to be eaten by the Tyrannosaurus Rex.

"You, the accused," the judge declared, "are found guilty of all the charges brought against you, and consequently, are sentenced to be sacrificed in the celebratory feast!"

The Velociraptors went wild, and Iron Butterfly's "You Can't Win," which had just finished, replayed from the top. Until the song slowed into its initial chorus, the Tyrannosaurus Rex banged his head while simultaneously using his tail to smack the gavel against the sound block. The Velociraptors started grooving with their tails, too, bringing them down against the base of the jury box like beavers.

"Order!" declared the judge once the song had slowed. "Task Force, begin the deliberation."

The Tyrannosaurus Task Force split into two lines, one on either side of the jury box. Both lines of jurors leaned forward, resting their snouts against the juror opposite them. The Velociraptors in one of the lines started shouting: "Appetizer! Appetizer! Appetizer!" The opposing line rebutted: "Dessert! Dessert! Dessert!" During this exchange, all the jurors' tails had been directed at Emma. They paused, shifted their tails to Colin, and proceeded with the deliberation. The first line of Velociraptors now shouted: "Dessert!" while the opposing line shouted back: "Appetizer!" After their rebuttal, the dinosaurs in the jury box left their lines and returned to their seats. Facing the Velociraptors, the Tyrannosaurus Rex raised the ridges above his eyes, and all the jurors nodded.

"Order!" the Tyrannosaurus Rex declared, slamming the gavel. "The deliberation is complete. The alien to be served as the celebratory appetizer is—"

A loud noise shot through the atmosphere as someone kicked the door down. Rose burst into the courtroom. Colin pinched his arm, winced. She had actually come back. She had decided to endanger her entire species for him. Despite his and Emma's verdict, he couldn't suppress the smile spreading across his face.

"Order in the court," wailed the Tyrannosaurus Rex, looking up at the courtroom's gilled rafters, refusing to bother with the visitor. "I will not tolerate any late witnesses. The intruder is now on trial!" He brought down the gavel without looking, missed the sound block by half a foot, but the jurors left their box and danced over to apprehend the Apatosaurus all the same. They hopped Rose to the defendants' table.

She sat beside Colin and curved her tail so that its tip rested in his hands underneath the table. He squeezed it. "How're you here?" he shouted over the music.

"I'll explain later."

"Order!" declared the Tyrannosaurus Rex, and as he brought down the gavel, he glanced at the new arrival for the first time. The mallet fell to the floor. His mouth hung open, but only silence came out. His eyes quickly darted from the defendants' table to the jury box, from Rose to the Velociraptors. To bring the judge back to the trial, one of the jurors danced over to the bench, used his or her tail to grab the gavel, and smacked the judge in the side of the head. The Velociraptor dropped the mallet on the bench and quickly retreated to the jury box. But before he or she could make it, the judge shouted, "Seize Velma!" and the other Velociraptors led her to the defendants' table. Velma sat beside Emma.

Iron Butterfly's "You Can't Win" restarted again, and as he had done the two previous times, the Tyrannosaurus Rex banged his head until the song entered its chorus. When it finally did, he shouted, "Order!" as he smacked the sound block with the gavel. "This is a historic day. Friends of the court," the jurors let loose a rehearsed hoot, "we have with us a special guest, an animal so rare that until this very moment, it was believed to have gone extinct ages ago. Today we have captured an Apatosaurus!"

"Objection," Rose shouted, rising into a four-footed two-step, upending the table in the process.

"Overruled," the judge declared.

"You did not capture me," Rose stated.

"Overruled!"

"And I watched you dance last night—"

"Silence!" shouted the Tyrannosaurus Rex.

"You're an awful dancer—"

"Jurors," the judge cried, "seize the Apatosaurus!"

The Velociraptors hopped out of their box and danced toward the defendants. Before they reached Rose, she challenged, "I doubt you'd last a single round against us in the Ultimate Dinosaur Dance-Off."

"Take her away!" the judge ordered, whacking the sound block.

As the Velociraptors led Rose out of the courtroom, she turned her neck toward the Tyrannosaurus Rex and shouted, "But if you win, I'll lead you to the Astral of the Apatosaurus."

"Jurors," the judge said, "just where do you think you're

going?"

"To the underground cell," one of the Velociraptors ventured.

"Imbeciles!" he shouted. "I was only trying to frighten the defendant. Bring her back to her seat at once, and while you're at it, fix the defendants' table. We must keep the courthouse clean."

Once the jurors had returned Rose and hopped back into their box, the Tyrannosaurus Rex asked, "What is this 'Astral' of which you speak?"

"It's a dimension between this one and the Astral Plane. It exists directly above the Northern Plains and only Apatosauruses can access it."

"Are you suggesting there are more of your kind in the Days of the Dinosaur?"

"Hundreds of us reside in the Astral of the Apatosaurus."

"And if I accept your challenge, you'll dance me to your Astral after I defeat you in the Ultimate Dinosaur Dance-Off?"

"Yes," said Rose, "you and your army."

"What're you bargaining for?"

"If we win," Rose said, "in addition to pardoning my crew from the champion's feast, which includes Colin, Emma, and Joe, you will let all dinosaur species coexist comfortably, just as they did in Prehistoric Paradise."

"Order in the court," the Tyrannosaurus Rex said, even though the room had already hushed, "we have reached a second verdict. I hereby accept the Apatosaurus's plea. She and the aliens will be sentenced to a round in the Ultimate Dinosaur Dance-Off. Task Force, escort the defendants to the Challengers' Quarters. And once they are settled, transfer the alien prisoner to their room as well."

The Velociraptors hopped to the defendants' table. Multiple tails wrapped around the prisoners' limbs, which included Velma. As the Tyrannosaurus Task Force hopped the challengers out of the courtroom, the judge declared, "Case dismissed!" and brought his gavel down for the final time.

Trillium Lake (Chapter Twenty-Five)

It was one of those rare autumn nights out on Trillium Lake. Northern Oregon had been hit by an October heat wave, and the weather hovered around the low seventies. The sky remained clear of clouds, and under a full moon and a sea of stars, Colin, Joe, and Emma floated on a wooden raft in the center of the lake. The night's natural light caused Mount Hood, which stood seven and a half miles to the north, to reflect in the water.

As Creedence Clearwater Revival's "Bad Moon Rising" came from Colin's portable boombox, which lay in the middle of the raft, Joe and Emma rose to their feet and danced. Colin sat beside the boombox, as they awkwardly collegiate shagged around him. He flinched into the fetal position as Joe and Emma's upper bodies pressed together, arching above him as their feet repeatedly kicked his sides.

"Come on," Joe said, planting a playful foot into Colin's left thigh, "dance with us."

Colin just sipped his beer and nodded along to the beat of the song.

"You'll never get better with your ass glued to the ground," Emma teased. Her voice descended onto Colin from above as she tapped his right thigh with her toes. "Besides, it's pretty dark, we'll hardly be able to see your mistakes."

He stayed silent as the song progressed into its course. Instead of trying to continue the conversation, Joe and Emma each grabbed one of Colin's hands and jerked him to his feet. They pulled his chest against theirs, and all three of them arched above the boombox. Together, they did a three-way shag, kicking their feet past the sides of the stereo, poking their toes through their partners' legs before sliding them back to their own corner of the triangle.

Joe had kept his left arm on Emma's hip while they shagged, and she had set her right hand on his shoulder. Colin remained the third wheel in this threesome, both his hands being held above his head by the boyfriend and girlfriend. As they gyrated around the boombox, they used their chests to keep each other from faceplanting onto the raft.

Colin started to feel less self-conscious as he danced with them. In addition to having just finished his midterms, he had submitted twenty applications to various graduate paleontology programs earlier in the week. Although he couldn't explain it, he knew he'd get into the University of Chicago. Consequently, once he graduated in a semester and a half, he'd be studying the remains of the only species he had ever wanted while attending his dream school. Maybe it had been because of this glorious gut feeling, or the fact that he had passed the point of being tipsy five beers ago, but for the first time since his mother had died, Colin allowed himself to get lost in the music and dance without restraint.

The Brothers Johnson's "Get the Funk Out Ma Face" replaced Creedence Clearwater Revival, and Colin broke away from the three-way collegiate shag. He placed his left hand on his hip, turned his body to his right, and stuck out his thumb. Then he repeated this move in the opposite direction. Under the influence of The Brothers Johnson, Colin performed the fiercest hitchhiker of his life. As Joe and Emma followed his lead, Mount Hood's aquatic reflection radiated throughout Trillium Lake. Besides his fantasies of getting intimate with an Apatosaurus, leading the two of them in this dance had been the most fulfilling moment of his life.

Reunion (Chapter Twenty-Six)

A VAST, CIRCULAR SPACE on the second floor of the House of Rex, the Challengers' Quarters stretched almost the entire length of the stipe. Diagonal gills, which waved up and down, covered its walls, creating the illusion that the room constantly spun counterclockwise. The sole source of light came from the corner of the room opposite the door, where Velma, the glowing Velociraptor, did a languid chicken dance. As Rose slid her tail into Colin's hands, he realized her height reached halfway to the ceiling, which stood approximately one mega-Apatosaurus tall. The ceiling's center dipped downward and glimmered gold as if it were a chandelier.

The door slid open and T. Rex's "Cosmic Dancer" permeated the Challengers' Quarters. The light increased significantly as a dozen members of the Tyrannosaurus Task Force led Joe into the room.

Emma immediately started leaping like a frog toward Joe, vaulting herself over the stooped backs of invisible friends while hiding her phantom limb behind her body. Joe slowly two-stepped away from the doorway, crossing his arms over his stomach, as if he were trying to conceal his brand new bulbous belly. It didn't help. If anything, it accentuated his additional body mass. Fat drooped over the waistline of his jeans and bounced whenever he shuffled his weight from one foot to the other. Even his face had become considerably chubbier. The Tyrannosaurus Task Force commanded Joe and Emma to halt, but neither listened, and the Velociraptors just shrugged. Amazed that Joe hadn't contracted any fatal infections, Colin simply stared at his brother. Emma leapt into Joe's arms, apparently unperturbed by his weight gain, and he caught her as if he were a hammock.

The Tyrannosaurus Task Force nodded at the light source on the other side of the room, and Velma returned the gesture. Then the Task Force left the challengers alone, and the sounds of "Cosmic Dancer" retreated with them. Once they had vanished, Joe noticed Emma's stump. He whispered something into her ear. She nodded. He bent his neck, and she slowly lifted her left arm. Joe repeatedly kissed the place where her hand had been. After a couple dozen kisses, she grinned. Emma told Joe that she loved him and missed him and would never let anything like this happen again. Then she asked him about his health.

As he two-stepped his girlfriend toward Colin, Joe said, "The dance across the island was hell. Halfway to the House of Rex, I became so sick I couldn't even stand, never mind dance. I don't know how long I was lying in the forest, but after a series of blackouts, the pain vanished. When I sat up, a couple of members of the Tyrannosaurus Task Force were still rubbing these strange branches all over my body."

"Calamite," Emma interjected.

Joe nodded. "This process happened a few times, and each spell of sickness hit me harder than the last. But then we finally made it to this mushroom, and ever since I arrived, I've felt fine."

Emma kissed him while she continuously apologized that she hadn't brought his antibiotics to save him from his sickness, told him she thought she'd never see him again, and she kissed him once more before they finally reached Colin and Rose. Colin now stood on his feet, performing the second most powerful sprinkler of his life. As Joe set Emma down, and Colin's right arm swung across his body in stop-motion, releasing invisible water into the room, he wrapped his appendage around Joe and embraced his brother.

Joe asked him where his shirt had gone, and Colin explained how it had been used as a tourniquet for Emma. Then Joe, looking over Colin's shoulder as they continued their hug, asked what had brought Velma to the Challengers' Quarters.

"She smacked the Tyrannosaurus Rex in the face with his gavel," Colin said, letting go of Joe, allowing his brother to drift back to Emma while his own hands reunited with Rose's tail. To avoid dancing, the four of them sat down.

Joe looked confused, but he simply nodded toward the Velociraptor in the corner of the room.

"Hey Joe," Velma called, and she started to float toward the group as she continued her chicken dance.

"You two know each other?" Emma sounded hurt.

"Yeah," Joe said nonchalantly, "she worked in the Dance Room across the hall from the Cesspool Cell while I was imprisoned." To Velma, he asked, "How was your first tour with the Task Force?"

"Terrible," she cried. "We barely made it out of the House of Rex before we found your friends. I'm so sorry."

Colin stared at Rose, whose scrunched up snout and slightly parted lips nearly mirrored his own.

When Velma reached the group, "Cosmic Dancer" lightly radiated from her body. Without standing, Joe introduced her to his friends, and then Colin introduced his brother to Rose. As he shook the Apatosaurus's tail, Joe lifted his eyebrows at Colin, who quickly shook his head, causing his twin to frown.

Once all the animals knew each other, Rose asked, "What's the Dance Room?"

"It's an underground chamber located in the stipe of the mushroom," Velma said, hovering over the group as her chicken dance continued. "It's where the young Velociraptors are stationed to dance before they are drafted into the Tyrannosaurus Task Force."

"But why have a Dance Room if everyone in the House of Rex is already dancing?" Colin asked.

"Because," Velma said, "the Dance Room is the only reason all the dinosaurs in the House of Rex still dance. After the Meteor of Mystical Movement caused the land to shake and this mushroom to grow, a state of subtle serenity momentarily spread throughout the island. This stillness caused the House of Rex to wilt and the recently genetically modified carnivores to revert to their natural state. To combat these reversions, the original

Tyrannosaurus Rex created the Dance Room, which in turn powered the Meteor of Mystical Movement."

"How?" Emma asked, her unharmed hand resting in Joe's lap.

"By continuous and decadent hardcore dancing," Joe said, reaching into Emma's lap with his free hand to cradle her stump.

"When the Velociraptors throw down," Velma said, "simultaneously punching the floor and kicking the walls of the Dance Room, they cause the mushroom's stipe to pulsate. And because the mushroom's stipe is connected to the Meteor of Mystical Movement deep within the island's core, their dance causes the meteor to send seismic ripples throughout the Days of the Dinosaur. These ripples, of course, are the reason all creatures on the island cannot help but dance."

"You mean," Rose said, her tail curling around Colin, "dance is the movement through which the carnivores are empowered, and yet, it is the only way we can free herbivore-kind?"

"Yes," Velma said.

Rose shook her head, and Colin kissed her coiling tail.

"Why're you telling us this?" Emma asked. "I mean, just hours ago, were you not with the Tyrannosaurus Task Force?"

"I was," Velma said.

"You captured Colin and I," Emma continued as Joe scooted closer to her, pressing his thigh against hers, "and then you sat on the jury that deliberated our sentence?"

"I did." Velma started to grind her beak back and forth, but the action seemed to be more of a nervous tic than a threat.

"So why are you acting as if you're against the Tyrannosaurus Rex all of a sudden?"

"I've been against the dictator for quite some time," the Velociraptor said. "The two members of the Task Force who were apprehended for mutiny, who were going to face the Tyrannosaurus Rex in his dance-off before the Apatosaurus revealed herself, are my best friends."

"So what?" Emma asked.

"So it's in her best interest to help us win," Joe said, leaning over to kiss Emma on her forehead.

"I already hated the Tyrannosaurus Rex for what he has done to my friends, which is motive enough to put me on your side. But now include my sentence, and with the exception of the Apatosaurus, we all face the same punishment. My survival is only possible through your success."

"What's going to happen to your friends now?" Colin asked.

"Mutiny is a crime against the Tyrannosaurus Rex," the Velociraptor said, sadly shaking her head. "They'll be executed tonight and served at the feast tomorrow."

"I'm so sorry," Rose said, and her eyes grew as wide as Colin's face. "I had no idea."

"It would have happened after the dance-off if you hadn't come along," Velma said. "Fodder had been their fate since they were arrested."

"What did they do?" Emma asked, suddenly sounding impressed.

"All they really did was refuse to whip Joe as he passed through his various death throes on their dance to the House of Rex. Instead of whipping him, they brought him calamite, which saved his life and allowed the Tyrannosaurus Rex to fatten your friend for the feast. But the dictator didn't see it like that. He sentenced them to a round of his Ultimate Dinosaur Dance-Off for their crimes, and losing the dance-off, which is inevitable, is itself a crime punishable by death."

"So your friends saved Joe just so he could be eaten by the Tyrannosaurus Rex?" Emma shouted.

"No," Joe said, and he leaned toward Emma and kissed her again. "They saved me to buy me some time before the dance-off. There are always challengers, and although it's practically impossible to defeat the Tyrannosaurus Rex in his dance-off, it's hypothetically possible. So being fattened for the feast was my best bet at surviving."

"Joe, you're sure we can trust her?" Emma squinted.

"Yeah," Joe said, nodding, "but it probably won't make much of a difference in the grand scheme of things."

"Why's that?" Colin asked.

The Velociraptor responded, "For a couple of decades, I've watched various creatures challenge the Tyrannosaurus Rex to his Ultimate Dinosaur Dance-Off, and without fail, they all lose."

"But," Colin asked, "did an Apatosaurus ever perform in the dance-off? They're by far the best dinosaur dancers on the island."

Rose tightened her tail around Colin's body. Her face glowed.

"Not since the original dance-off," Velma said. "But it doesn't matter how talented the challengers are because any animal can out-dance the current Tyrannosaurus Rex. He's literally the worst dancer on the island. But it's impossible to win the Ultimate Dinosaur Dance-Off because the Tyrannosaurus Rex is the primary judge, and he'll always declare himself the winner. In order to survive, the challengers will have to not only defeat the dictator in his dance-off, but will have to kill him and his army afterwards as well, which is impossible."

"But the prophecy states," Rose interjected, "if the challengers choose the right dance, they will summon Bau from the sky, who, in turn, will restore Prehistoric Paradise."

"Throughout history, nearly all challengers have claimed such, and they're all convinced they know the correct dance, too. But now virtually every dance has been performed in the dance-off, and the challengers are still always eaten."

Colin, Rose, Emma, and Joe sat in silence while Velma floated overhead. "Cosmic Dancer" drizzled down from the Velociraptor's body. As the song finished and then restarted, Joe asked, "Have any of the challengers tried the Grand Break?"

Colin's eyes widened. He looked at Joe and shook his head.

Rose asked, "What's that?"

Joe smiled. "The winning dance."

"Maybe," Emma said, "except it's impossible. Anyone who has tried it has ended up hospitalized or dead."

"How is it performed?" Rose asked.

"The Grand Break begins with a handless headspin," Colin said, unsure why he felt the need to explain the move that killed his mom to his dream dinosaur. Uncomfortably, he continued, "From there, the dancer places their hands on their hips and spins them as hard as they can in the opposite direction of their body. This dislocates the hips and causes the lower half of the body to actually spin in the opposite direction of the upper half, splitting the body in two for a single rotation before the dancer catches their hips and sets them back into place."

"It sounds like our best option," Velma said.

"How can you say that?" Emma asked. "It's not even possible."

"Maybe not," the Velociraptor said, "but no dancer has tried it in the dance-off before. So if we can pull it off, the Grand Break just might work."

"There's only one problem," Joe said, smiling at his friend. "I would try it, but I'm way too fat to dance like that."

"Why're you looking at me?" Colin asked, trying to redirect his brother's gaze by staring at Emma.

"Because you're going to perform the Grand Break."

Colin laughed, unsure if Joe were being serious. "If it almost killed you, how could I possibly perform it? I've never even done a headspin in my life, never mind a handless one. I mean, Emma's way more prepared."

"It can't be her," Joe said. "The move is only possible if the performer has complete trust in an Apatosaurus, and given Emma's family history with animals, well, it just has to be you."

"What about my family history with this stupid dance move?" Colin asked.

"Part of the reason it has to be you is because of your history. Mom invented it, so it's only right that you save dinosaurkind, the only species you've ever truly desired, with the Grand Break."

Colin nodded. He had to admit that it certainly seemed like the perfect way to woo Rose.

"And don't worry about the headspin," Joe added, "we'll teach you how to do that."

"Yeah," Emma agreed. "They aren't that difficult."

"But my biceps," Colin protested. He flashed both his biceps but refused to flex. "I'm way too weak to split my body in half."

"It doesn't matter how strong you are," Joe said. "Even if your biceps were as big as mom's at the end of her life, you'd share the same fate. Even if you could use your strength to spin your lower body counter to your headspin, you wouldn't be able to rotate fast enough to complete the Grand Break."

"So why bother with the move at all?"

"Because since we came to the Days of the Dinosaur, since I've been locked in the Cesspool Cell, I've had plenty of long hours to meditate on why the Grand Break almost killed me, and I think I've figured out a solution that will make the dance potentially possible. With Rose by your side, and the speed with which she can snap her tail, she'll be able to dislocate the lower half of your body, spin it, and catch it quicker than any human alive. You're the only one who can do this dance, Colin, because no one else knows and trusts Rose like you."

Colin looked at Rose, fearing she'd be on board with what would likely be his cause of death, but, at the same time, kind of hoping she'd be willing to undergo this intimate experience with him. If she were willing to split him in half, what else would she be willing to do to him? What would this mean for their relationship? She just squeezed his whole body with her coiling tail. He smiled weakly, and shivers danced down his spine.

Training Preview (Chapter Twenty-Seven)

COLIN HELD A HANDSTAND as "Walk the Dinosaur" by Was (Not Was) boomed throughout the Challengers' Quarters. Joe's fingers clasped around Colin's ankles, keeping him from tipping over. Slowly, Joe released his grip. As he stepped back, Colin fell to the floor.

"It's useless," Colin cried, lying on his back. He wished Rose and Velma would do something besides two-step behind him, studying his every move. Even though he appreciated hearing the Apatosaurus's encouragement, it made him extra self-conscious. "This is the song's fourth cycle, and I'm as terrible as ever."

"You're getting better," Joe said, grabbing Colin's ankles and lifting him into another handstand, acting as if he didn't notice the dinosaurs in the room. "It hasn't even been fifteen minutes and you're already able to hold your handstand for a few seconds without my help."

"Really?" Colin asked, standing upside-down, surprised.

"Yeah," Joe said, who had already let go of Colin. "And you've been standing by yourself for at least a half-dozen seconds now."

Colin shook his legs lightly and discovered the reality of the situation for himself. He grinned, and a few seconds later, toppled over.

"See," Joe said, "it's easy. Just don't overthink it. This time try getting into position on your own."

On Colin's first attempt, he kicked off the ground too gently and only rose into a right angle before his feet returned to the floor. In his next effort, he overcompensated, rotating past the point of a vertical line before crashing down onto his back. During his third attempt, he found a balance and propelled his body into a linear handstand. He held it for thirty seconds before landing on his feet.

"Great," Joe said, clapping Colin on the back, "now do it two more times before we work on turning this into a headspin."

Once Colin felt confident in his ability to handstand, he sat on the mushroom floor and plucked a piece of cauliflower from his pants. He bit into it, but instantly vomited as the salty flavor of stale urine blitzed his brain. He inspected the rest of the cauliflower in his hand, which had turned dark yellow. He threw the vegetable aside and regretted peeing his pants in the presence of the Tyrannosaurus Rex.

He asked Emma for something to eat. She sat at the tip of the triangle, and Joe occupied the side opposite him. She tossed Colin a head of cabbage that she had pulled from her pants. He could taste her sweat as he chewed, but her perspiration had a far more tolerable flavor than the urine-soaked vegetables in his own pants. After Colin had finished his snack, he continued training.

Following Joe's lead, Colin ran in place, and as they sprinted side by side, loosening up their muscles, they watched Emma stand on her head, balancing herself with her single hand.

"See how she twists her hips back and forth?" Joe asked, pointing to Emma, who straightened out her right leg before her body while bending her left leg behind her.

Colin nodded, and his running man started to wane.

"And once she feels comfortable twisting her hips, all she has to do is continue to twist them in the same direction in order to spin her body." As Joe spoke, Emma started to rotate to her right, twisting her handstand into a headspin. "Why don't you give it a whirl?"

Colin bent over, placed his hands and the crown of his head against the mushroom floor, and lifted himself into a handstand. He closed his eyes and pretended he went back in time to his childhood bedroom with his mother while she still lived. Under the guidance of her voice, he twisted his hips from side to side, and once he could move his legs flawlessly, he began to rotate. He fell immediately. He tried again. This time he imagined his mother's hands aiding his rotation, and he completed half a circle before crashing. As Colin continued to practice his breakdance, improving the length of his spin with every additional effort, "Walk the Dinosaur" replayed endlessly.

Eventually, Colin performed the first headspin of his life, rotating again and again and again. Joe called Rose over, and Colin's mother evaporated from his mind. Upside-down, he saw Rose two-step toward him in flashes, her body a blur as the dizziness started to set in. By the time she reached his side, he couldn't differentiate between colors, and her body had blended with the rest of the room. He heard Joe coaching the Apatosaurus on how to use her tail to dislocate Colin's hips, how to split his body in half.

Colin wondered if the performance would hurt. He knew the logic behind the Grand Break followed Newton's third law of motion. If the force disconnecting the lower body from the upper body used enough strength and speed, the lower body's reaction would match the force of the initial action, and hypothetically, this would cause the dislocation to happen so swiftly that it would be over almost before it began. Somehow, this also meant that the process would be painless, but Colin couldn't remember what specifically created this correlation. From his mother's onstage screams and his brother's hospitalization, pain clearly presented itself when the procedure went wrong. But what if the pain they had experienced affected him for the half-second his body had split? What if the pain felt so unbearable that, even if he managed to pull off the Grand Break, his mind became permanently paralyzed?

Colin's worries withered as Rose wrapped her tail around his spinning body, and she flipped him into an upright position. As the nausea from his dance dissipated, Emma and Velma joined the rest of the crew in the center of the room. Colin and the challengers formed a circle while Joe started to outline their moves for the portion of their performance preceding the Grand Break. Once the dancers understood the choreography, they resumed their rehearsal for the Ultimate Dinosaur Dance-Off. As the sun outside began its descent, the light shining through the mushroom walls slowly dimmed.

The Traceosaurus (Chapter Twenty-Eight)

COLIN LOST HIS VIRGINITY two weeks into his relationship with Tracey. They had just returned to his dorm room after finishing their first Introduction to Geology exam. Joe and Emma would be in one of their dance classes for the next couple of hours, and since Colin and Tracey had been up all night studying for the test, they had planned to take a long nap before he had to leave for Statistics in the evening. When they entered his room, he told Tracey he'd meet her in bed after he took a quick detour to the toilet.

When Colin walked into his blanket fort, Led Zeppelin's "Whole Lotta Love" roared from the small stereo on his nightstand, and he immediately abandoned any notion of napping. Tracey lounged across the width of the bed, her head tilted to her right and her eyes intensely fixed on Colin's hips as she rested on all fours. She licked her lips.

While Colin used the bathroom, Tracey had somehow painted her face so that it resembled an Apatosaurus-human hybrid. Besides the belt she had strapped around her waist, which sported a tail that dangled down her backside, she stripped naked. Before Colin could take off his shirt, his penis pulsated. Before he had taken off his pants, pre-come had already coated his cock.

Tracey lifted a hand and used her middle finger to beckon

Colin toward her. He reached the bed in a single stride and knelt down to press his lips against hers. Tracey intercepted the kiss with her palm before stretching her neck until it brushed against his ear. She whispered that they were animals, that she wanted his tongue inside her. Before Colin could respond, she turned around on the bed until her butt greeted him. Colin sat on the astroturf floor with his back against the bed, and once he had tilted his head so it rested atop the comforter, Tracey sat on his face.

As Colin wedged his tongue past her pubic hair, past both layers of labia, burrowing it as deep as it would dive, he stroked Tracey's plush tail. After a few minutes of soaking in his girlfriend's fluids, Colin pulled her by the plushy appendage, scooting Tracey an inch lower on his face, and he began to drag his tongue across her clitoris. Her breathing became heavy and rapid, and as "Whole Lotta Love" came to a close, she moaned. The Shadows of Knight's "Gloria" replaced Led Zeppelin's song, and Tracey lifted herself off Colin. Resting on her hands and knees once more, she elevated her butt in the air.

Colin sprung to his feet, lifted her tail so that it rested on his shoulder, and slowly slid himself inside the Traceosaurus. As he thrust his hips back and forth, he resumed stroking his girlfriend's tail. And the second he curved the plush tip into his mouth, he came. Colin moaned as he continued to suck on her tail, serenely rocking himself inside her, depositing his last few drops.

Once he pulled out, Colin and Tracey collapsed into bed, two fallen branches lying side by side. Her tail poked through his legs and rested just beneath his balls. He kissed the back of her head as he caressed her breast, and Tracey confessed that this had been the best sex she'd ever had. She said pretending to be a dinosaur had heightened everything about the act. With nothing to compare it to, Colin had to agree.

But as they spooned in his bed post-coital, Colin imagined he cuddled with an Apatosaurus.

Night Reframed (Chapter Twenty-Nine)

ALONG THE BACK WALL OF THE CHALLENGERS' QUARTERS, lit by the faint glow of the Velociraptor, Joe, Emma, and Velma appeared to be asleep. Joe snored, and Emma and Velma had been still for quite some time. Under Colin's arms, Rose's tail spiraled around his body, and he held its tip in his hands, resting against it like a pillow.

Colin had been flooded by questions ever since Rose had burst into the courtroom. He wanted to know if she had left him the night before because, like Emma had suggested, she was only supposed to guide them to the outskirts of the House of Rex. If so, did she only desert him for that reason, or did it have something to do with their kiss? Did she like kissing him? Did she kick down the courtroom door because she wanted to kiss him again? And this time, would she want to do more than just kiss? But more than anything, he wanted to know if her appearance in the courtroom, her challenge against the Tyrannosaurus Rex, meant that she loved him. Until this moment, when Joe and Emma were drifting through dreams, Colin had failed to find a single second where he could escape his crew to converse with Rose alone.

But now, as they lay together in the dark, his chance had finally come. Without turning to face the Apatosaurus, he whispered, "Rose? You awake?"

"Yes," she whispered back.

Colin froze. He couldn't convince his mouth to create words.

"Is everything all right?" Rose asked.

"Yeah," Colin croaked. He cleared his throat and chose the first question that came to mind. "Why'd you come back for us?"

"I was assigned the task of getting you and Emma into the Ultimate Dinosaur Dance-Off," Rose said, "and I thought you could use some help."

"Your job was to guide us to the House of Rex, wasn't it?" Colin asked, fidgeting with the tip of her tail. "Not to risk your entire species' extinction by revealing yourself to the Tyrannosaurus Rex. If any of the other guides had done what you've done, you never would have been hatched."

"I admit," Rose said, laying her head down beside Colin, "I might have taken some liberties with my assignment."

"But if you had already completed it, why'd you dance into the courtroom?"

"Because," Rose said, squeezing his body tight with her tail, "I couldn't dance the rest of my life knowing I'd never see you again, knowing that I'd left you to die."

Colin sucked in his cheeks and chomped, turning his face into a fish. Beadlets of blood trickled across his tongue. Regardless, he grinned. Rose's feelings for him were genuine.

"Colin?" Rose asked. "What're you doing?"

"Uh," he stammered, "nothing. I'm sorry. Rose," he said, squeezing the tip of her tail, "I'm crazy about you."

Rose smiled weakly, "I'm crazy about you, too."

"Really?" Colin asked, elated.

"Really," Rose said, "no one has ever risked their life for me by promising to try the Grand Break before."

Colin nodded. He grinned and gulped.

"And I want you to know that I really do care about you. But," Rose said, staring at Colin sternly, "you also need to know that we'll never be able to mate singularly. Believe me, I want to, it's just too selfish."

Colin sighed, disappointed. Still, Rose had returned, had risked the extinction of her species for no other reason than to be by his side. "I understand," he said, "and I'd never be able to live with myself if you became DinoManic over me." He brought the tip of her tail to his lips and kissed it for a long time. He continued, "I want you to know that if we live long enough to see Prehistoric Paradise, we don't need to be mates. As long as we get to be around each other, as long as I can hold your tail in my hand, I'll be the happiest animal in the kingdom."

"Do you mean that?" Rose asked, glowing. "You'd be happy in my presence even if I mated with other dinosaurs?"

"I think so," Colin murmured, looking at the floor.

"Are you sure?" Rose asked, hopeful.

"Yes," Colin said, confident. After all, just because Rose copulated with other Apatosauruses didn't mean she wanted to sleep with them. Besides, anatomically speaking, he still had no idea how mating with his dream dinosaur would work.

Rose used her tail to bring Colin toward her mouth and washed his face with a single lick. Before she could bathe him again, Colin placed his hands on both sides of her snout and pressed his lips against hers. Rose kissed him back, but before the desire to slide his tongue into her mouth overpowered him, Colin tilted his head away.

"We can't," Colin said, his whole body tingling. "What if you become DinoManic?"

Though she looked like she tried to contain it, Rose laughed.

"What's so funny?" Colin asked, his face burning bright red as if he were impersonating the Tyrannosaurus Rex.

"I'm sorry," Rose said, controlling her laughter, "but Colin, just because we can't mate singularly doesn't mean we can't mate at all."

"Really?" Colin exclaimed.

"Yeah," Rose said, "and I don't see any reason why we shouldn't mate freely right now. Unless, of course, you don't want to?"

Colin returned his hands to Rose's snout and pressed his mouth against her colorful lips. Their tongues met between her teeth, and as the dreamy taste of lukewarm lettuce consumed him, Love's "She Comes in Colors" boomed throughout the circular room. They spent a few minutes engaged in an intense tongue war, slamming their moist members together, trying to pin down their opponent. But before she could be declared the victor, Rose withdrew her tongue and separated herself from Colin. He stared into her eyes and smiled wide, and the Apatosaurus rolled over onto her back.

Rose's tail still coiled around Colin, and she held him away from her body as she flipped over, protecting him from a potential pulping. Once she completed her rotation, she set him down on her stomach before unraveling her tail. He began kissing her belly as he crawled up her body. "She Comes in Colors" had played all the way through by the time he made it to the base of her neck. As the song reset, he stuck out his tongue and started his ascent, licking the entire length of her neck before their mouths met. She slid her tail down the back of his pants, stroking his bare bottom as they swapped interspecial spit. His hands massaged the sides of her snout.

Rose struggled removing his pants. She kept pulling at the back of his waistband, but they wouldn't budge. He kissed her again before sliding down her neck onto her stomach. Colin stood and started two-stepping on the Apatosaurus's belly as he unbuckled his belt, and Rose stretched her neck through her front legs and licked his body from his waist to his face.

Once the belt had been unbuckled, Colin lay on his back, and Rose bit the cuff of his pants. She yanked off his jeans and the few remaining vegetables tumbled down her body before falling to the mushroom floor. Next Rose removed his underwear, and once she tossed them aside, she licked his toes, his shins, his knees. Slowly, she made her way up his thighs, and the instant her tongue touched his cock, he came. The Apatosaurus lapped up his semen before continuing her course toward his mouth.

The flavor of lukewarm lettuce now contained a slight hint of salt, and Colin wondered how he could possibly return the favor. Did she get off from penetration? And if she did, how could he possibly please her? How could he possibly fill the void of an Apatosaurus? Rose pushed her tongue into his mouth, and as Colin gagged, he wiggled his body from side to side, slowly shimmying down the dinosaur's belly. He raised his hands above his head and caressed the Apatosaurus's flesh, searching for an opening.

When Rose's hind legs leaked into his peripheral vision, and he still hadn't found her cloaca, Colin started to worry. What if he couldn't find it? Worse, what if he'd already passed her orifice and had failed to realize it? Before he reached the base of her tail, Rose placed her mouth over his hands. Biting gently, she lifted him off her body and set him on the floor.

When his feet touched the gilled ground, Colin lifted his right leg and extended it in a straight line behind his body, balancing on a stiff left leg. He smiled up at Rose, wondering why she had stopped kissing him, why she had set him on the ground, why she had risen to her feet, but her shimmy turned her away from him, and he could no longer see her face.

As he held his arabesque, his erection began to subside. He had failed to find her cloaca, and now Rose wouldn't even look at him. He wished he'd had just a little more time. He felt confident he had almost found it, but now he had lost his opportunity. He looked at the floor, afraid of the expression he'd see if the dinosaur curved her face toward him.

But before his penis fell completely flaccid, he felt Rose's tail wrap around his body, further securing his statuesque arabesque. Automatically, he looked in the direction from which the contact came, and the dinosaur smiled down at him.

"Don't worry," Rose said softly, dragging him toward her. "This won't hurt, I promise."

"What won't hurt?" Colin asked, confused.

"It will be better if I just show you," Rose said. "Put your hands together and lift your arms above your head."

"Like this?" Colin asked, his erection returning as he raised his arms as if he were preparing to dive into the deep end of a swimming pool.

"Perfect," Rose said, pulling him between her hind legs.

The Apatosaurus hovered above him. As she lifted up her backside, Colin finally discovered her cloaca directly overhead, located halfway between the base of Rose's tail and her hind legs. The outer lips shared the same green, purple, and blue tie-dye hues as the rest of her skin. But as she swayed above him, her lips folded outward, revealing a tire-sized crater of neon pink flesh. She grew engorged, coated in rainbow fluid, which glimmered in the faint glow of the Velociraptor from the other side of the room. Fist-sized drops of cloacal fluid slowly dripped onto Colin's chest, covering him with an odor akin to steamed cabbage. He nibbled on his lower lip, trying to replace desire with pain to prolong his approaching orgasm.

"I love you!" Rose shouted.

Before Colin could respond, before he could even process Rose's exclamation, the Apatosaurus sat down, and his hands disappeared inside the dinosaur. He opened his mouth to ask about her sudden descent, but before the words could escape, her neon pink flesh had swallowed his head, and he suffocated on her cloacal fluids. She inhaled his hips, and Colin gulped her liquid rainbows, savoring the taste of warm leafy oysters sliding down his throat. As the dinosaur absorbed his ankles, and his feet fluttered their way inside, he thought about what she had said: Rose the Apatosaurus loved him.

When he entered Rose, her wet flesh clung to his skin as he crawled through a neon pink corridor that had the circumference of a vinyl record. Cloacal fluids filled his nostrils, and when he opened his mouth to breathe, he choked. After slurping down her secretions, he kept his mouth closed, held his breath. He wondered how long her flesh would cling to him, worried it would never cease. What if he got stuck? What if this portal never ended? What if he died drowning on their love? But shortly after her lips closed around his feet, his fingers broke through the end of her fleshy tunnel, and his body quickly followed. He slid into a cavity shaped like a Deinonychus-sized raindrop and belly-flopped into a puddle of fluid.

Inside Rose's cloacal chamber, Colin stood and two-stepped, brushing his back against her flesh wall and sloshing around her secretions. The opening from which he had plunged into this cavity occupied the space behind his coccyx. The hole had shrunk to the size of a compact disc, and the dinosaur's cloacal fluids had coagulated across the orifice. Hanging in the center of the chamber, a rainbow-colored egg sac strobed, flashing light against the neon pink flesh surrounding it. Could this dangling bulb be a cloacal clitoris? Yes! As Colin looked up at it, the rainbow clitoris vibrated like stereo speakers, and the sounds of Love's "She Comes in Colors" significantly increased.

To keep himself from slipping on Rose's secretions, Colin performed the most cautious electric slide of his life as he grooved toward the bulb. After a few slides, he reached the center of the chamber and danced directly beneath the dinosaur's egg sac. He raised his arms and latched onto it, lifting himself into the air. As his body brushed against the flashing bulb, the Apatosaurus moaned.

The texture reminded Colin of a leather couch cushion. He climbed up her clitoris until his head bumped into the ceiling of

Rose's cloacal chamber. He wrapped his arms and legs around her egg sac, squeezing it in a full-body embrace while he rubbed himself against her in rhythm to Love's song. Her moans remained soft, and they started to match his body's brief ascents. But when his penis accidentally penetrated the soft rainbow skin, the chamber quaked, and fluid started to seep from the walls. The puddle beneath him rose rapidly as he humped the Apatosaurus's clitoris, and he started to bang his head against the base of her bulb whenever the light strobed. Her moans grew louder as the puddle became a pool, and the pace of Colin's hips quickened.

Rose's fluids reached his feet and continued to rise. They crept up his thighs. As the liquid passed his waist he licked the clitoris. The taste of her stringy rainbows danced along his tongue, and he suctioned his lips around the dinosaur's flesh. He sucked in some of her egg sac as the cloacal fluids reached his chest. With each thrust, the liquids splashed onto the underside of his chin. His moans matched those of the Apatosaurus. As her secretions crept above his lower lip, he gargled the warm fluids.

Colin kept gulping as he sucked on her rainbow flesh while the secretions swallowed his head, distorting the sounds of the song and the dinosaur's moans. As he suffocated on Rose's cloacal fluids, he shot his seed inside her, and the Apatosaurus came, too, which caused the thin layer of flesh covering her compact disc orifice to crack. As Colin convulsed, the fluid filling her cloacal chamber flushed out, and the current carried him into her hole, which had grown to the size of a vinyl record once more. Colin darted through the fleshy portal and torpedoed out of the dinosaur's cloaca.

He dove toward the gilled floor of the Challengers' Quarters, but before he crashed, Rose caught him with her tail and curled it around his body. The Apatosaurus collapsed to the floor and lay on her side. She set him down, his back resting against her belly, and curved her tail and neck until they met between her front and hind legs. Colin grinned as the Apatosaurus enveloped him, and Rose returned the gesture before nuzzling her head against his chest.

The Ultimate Dinosaur Dance-Off (Chapter Thirty)

COLIN AND THE REST OF THE CHALLENGERS two-stepped on the top floor of the House of Rex. They were in a cylindrical tube with a circumference half the size of the stipe. The gilled ground in the tube began to rise, and the ceiling above them started to slide open. Sunlight peered into the room and Rose shoved the tip of her tail into Colin's hand as they made their gradual ascent. He squeezed her affectionately and wished they could relive the previous night again and again. But before his erection could rise past half-mast, Beck's "Loser" reverberated throughout the cylinder, blaring from the dance-floor overhead.

The sunbeams were too bright for Colin to see anything past the half-open hatch, and he quickly quit trying to glimpse what lay ahead. Joe and Emma were enlaced, and Velma sniffled. Beside him, Rose quivered. As Colin continued his two-step in the rising room, he feared being feast food. What if he couldn't execute the Grand Break? What if, after splitting him in half, Rose could not put him back together again? But even if Joe were right, and Rose's assistance somehow allowed Colin to pull off the Grand Break, would it actually change their situation? If the manner in which the Tyrannosaurus Rex judged their trial indicated how he would judge his Ultimate Dinosaur Dance-Off, they couldn't possibly win. And without the divine help of a mystical being like Bau, he doubted they'd be able to usurp the

Tyrannosaurus Rex. Colin hoped Emma had been wrong about the Apatosauruses fabricating the prophecy, about the story of Bau being complete crap.

As the chorus of Beck's "Loser" chimed throughout the arena, the challengers' heads peeked past the opening to the dance-floor, and the audience assaulted Colin and his crew with a cacophony of boos. The crowd consisted of four differing dinosaur species. Velociraptors, Piratops, and Astralsauruses filled the stands around the perimeter of the mushroom's vibrating cap, stands that must have been built overnight, while Discodactyls hovered overhead. A clear tarp had been erected around the arena, shielding the dancers as well as the audience members from falling objects, causing the Discodactyls' snow to slide harmlessly to the floor on the outskirts of the House of Rex. The three types of creatures in the stands were sectioned off according to species. The Astralsauruses sat behind the antipodal point where the challengers two-stepped, or, at least Colin assumed they were sitting—he couldn't say for sure because only their floating eyes were visible above the seats. On either side of the Astralsauruses, members of the Tyrannosaurus Task Force squatted. And on the opposite end of the dance-floor, beyond the place where the Tyrannosaurus Rex's presence would soon appear, Piratops had settled into their extra wide seats. Under the guidance of three Velociraptors, who sat behind a table at the base of the stands to the challengers' left and who held signs that boldly stated **BOO**, the crowd continued to show their contempt for Colin's crew.

The instant "Loser" ended, Queen's "We Will Rock You" replaced it. The intensity of the cap's quakes increased dramatically, and the three Velociraptors lifted signs that proclaimed **CHEER**. Every dinosaur in the stands stomped along to the song. Additionally, the Astralsauruses blinked with vigor, the Velociraptors did somersaults as they floated above their seats, and the Piratops sharpened the three tie-dye sabers protruding from their heads by rubbing them together, which caused the colorful parrots to squawk. Even the Discodactyls shining in the sky flapped their wings a little faster.

The Tyrannosaurus Rex's boiling red head poked out of the opening in the center of the stipe as Queen's song entered its initial chorus. Somehow, the cheers from the crowd doubled in volume as the Tyrannosaurus Rex, whose whole head had now emerged into view, roared the song's lyrics. The dictator's horizontal body surfaced, and he began to jerk his swamp-green backside from one side to the other each time the dinosaurs in the stands stomped their feet. He tried to clap his golden, wing-shaped arms along with the crowd and the song, but they only made it about a quarter of the way across his chest before silently bouncing off his body. The inability to clap didn't deter his determination. As he strenuously stretched his feathery arms, his red head started to sweat. When his feet finally emerged onto the dance-floor, the Tyrannosaurus Rex started stomping them twice as hard as any dinosaur in attendance, as if he were compensating for the shortcomings of his arms.

Once the Tyrannosaurus Rex had roared the chorus for the final time, and the guitar took control of the song, the returning champion pumped his tiny arms up and down and sprinted around the circumference of the dance-floor. The three Velociraptors in charge of the signs lifted the word **WAVE** into the air. As the dictator ran around the arena, the dinosaurs in the audience jumped to their feet and wildly flung their arms above their heads. The Tyrannosaurus Rex made two complete loops around the arena before "We Will Rock You" came to a close, and then he returned to the center of the dance-floor.

The Velociraptors' sign now said **SILENCE** as the Tyrannosaurus Rex cleared his throat, preparing to make a speech. Colin's crew appeared timid, and he wanted to say something encouraging to pump up his team during this pre-speech silence, but every sentiment he imagined himself saying seemed insufficient. Rose pulled her tail out of his hand. For a split second he felt doomed. But then she wrapped it around his body and pulled him close to her front legs. She curved her neck until her mouth rested against his ear and whispered that everything would be all right, that she wouldn't let him die doing the Grand Break. Colin bent his head and kissed the tip of the Apatosaurus's tail, which rested beneath his chin, and he confessed to Rose that no matter what happened during the dance-off, the dinosaur of his dreams being by his side made him the happiest human alive.

Before Rose could respond, the Tyrannosaurus Rex began his speech with a roar. "Three hundred and nineteen years ago, a

Tyrannosaurus Rex called Tuque freed all carnivores from the herbivore lifestyle via the power of dance." He paused to appreciate the audience as they applauded him. "On that same day, he became the first champion of the Ultimate Dinosaur Dance-Off!" The Tyrannosaurus Rex waited for more applause, but none came. Annoyed, he repeated the phrase, "first champion of the Ultimate Dinosaur Dance-Off!" and this time the three Velociraptors remembered to raise the sign pronouncing **APPLAUSE**. Once the audience had hushed again, and the three Velociraptors on sign duty had been arrested and replaced, the Tyrannosaurus Rex continued. "In the dance-off debut, Tuque defeated the creatures who created the laws that starved his sole-mate Sue and their precious offspring. He defeated multiple members of the most diet-restrictive species of all time: The Apatosaurus." The Tyrannosaurus Rex paused again to survey the audience. The dinosaurs in the stands seemed to be impressed by his ancestor's historic feat.

"But now, exactly three hundred and nineteen years after Tuque freed carnivore-kind, the Apatosaurus is once again attempting to confine connoisseurs of meat." Contemptuous chants circulated throughout the arena. Over the boos of the crowd, the Tyrannosaurus Rex promised, "Today, three hundred and nineteen years later, I, in the tradition of Tuque, will preserve our diet! After I defeat the challengers, they will guide us to a plane of existence overflowing with voluptuous vegetable eaters where we will recapture the creatures who want to take away our freedom to pursue a leafless lifestyle. Once we have restored the Apatosauruses to the Cesspool Cell, they will create more than enough fodder to feed every carnivore on the island!"

To silence the audience's applause, the Tyrannosaurus Rex tilted his stubby arms toward the sky, lifting them as high as he could. "But in order to feast," the dictator declared, "the Ultimate Dinosaur Dance-Off must have a champion." The Tyrannosaurus Rex turned in circles as he pumped his winged-arms, only two-stepping in place once all the dinosaurs on the mushroom had risen to their feet. "And before I'm the champion, what must we do?"

Under the directive of the Velociraptors' sign, the crowd cried, "Dance!" Instantly, David Bowie's "Let's Dance" aired throughout the arena. As the Tyrannosaurus Rex sashayed toward his side of the mushroom, the challengers circled around Colin.

"Don't let the crowd get you down," Velma said. "Most of them would be rooting for us if their lives weren't on the line."

"Really?" Rose asked. She sounded shocked.

"Yeah," Velma replied, "I always secretly cheered for the challengers, and I wasn't the only one. The problem is, there's no way to know which Velociraptors will turn you in for having mutinous intent, so no dinosaur on the Task Force talks."

"The crowd's on our side," Colin said, bringing the conversation back to the challenge before them. "And the fate of dinosaurkind is in our feet. Is everybody ready to dance?" Colin sounded more hyped than he felt.

His crew simultaneously replied in the affirmative.

"Are you ready?" Rose excitedly asked, squeezing him with her tail for reassurance.

Colin nodded. As David Bowie's song came to a close, he said, "Let's dance!"

Pink Floyd's "Interstellar Overdrive" blasted through the arena, cancelling out the noise of the crowd, and Colin's crew started to dance toward the center of the wavy cap. They followed him as he spun in slow circles, his bones absorbing the mushroom's vibrations, which caused his body to shake like Jell-O.

His team reached the middle of the dance-floor thirty seconds later where their spins gained speed in sync with the song. The stipe convulsed every couple of seconds, sending massive ripples throughout the cap. Each time the challengers surged toward the crest of a wave, they used the momentum to catapult themselves into the air where they performed exquisite *tours en l'air.* The wave caught them as it sunk to its trough before quickly sending them skyward once more. Colin and his crew continued their ballet as the sounds of the song became increasingly sporadic. As the tempo abated, the frequency of the waves decreased, and the challengers' *tours en l'air* slowed like a climatic clap. Once the song lost all its gravity, the dancers split up their circle.

Emma and Velma flipped onto their heads and spun toward the Tyrannosaurus Rex at snail speed while Joe began to do the worm between them. Colin grabbed Rose's snout with his left hand and her tail with his right. The Apatosaurus lifted her partner into the air, and they rotated toward the other side of the cap. Despite everything they had been through, his stomach still fluttered like it had during their psychedelic swing. As the dancers continued to groove away from the cap's center, their pace gradually increased. But when they reached opposite ends of the dance-floor, their movements suddenly reverted to slow motion.

The hump of each wave now came thirty seconds apart. Every time a ripple's crest rolled under Colin and Rose, the Apatosaurus swung him through her front and hind legs, tossing him high into the air once he had cleared the width of her belly. He weightlessly soared over his partner as if he were a dinosaur somersaulting from one spiraled neck to the next during the Apatosaurus Quadrille. As his ascension peaked, Rose retracted her head and tail from between her legs, and without losing momentum, swung them over her body. She caught Colin as she sunk into the mushroom trench. Her neck and tail wrapped around his hands, holding him like a cross as he hovered over the hump. When the wave lifted Rose back toward the crest, she repeated this process in reverse.

For roughly four minutes, Colin and Rose repeated this pattern as they danced in slow motion. They completed a full aerial figure eight every sixty seconds. After they finished the first figure eight, their presence started to lag. As they entered their second swing, their bodies resembled a long-exposure photograph, a blurry figure eight frozen in the dance-floor frame. It became impossible to follow their dance during the final two figures. Their bodies had become a complex web of cloudy color, and Colin felt as if he were buffering.

But after the fourth figure, when the tempo of the song aired out, Rose tossed Colin with all her strength, breaking the image of the infinite eight. He flew through the air at turtle speed. As he sailed skyward, his body performed acrobatic flips. When he faced the dance-floor, he watched Rose jump over a rope formed by her neck and tail. She left her feet whenever a wave peaked. On the other side of the mushroom's cap, Emma and Velma did a slow motion headspin beside each other, completing a rotation as often as Colin finished a flip. Joe did the lazy worm at the top of the triangle, lying flat on his stomach and languidly rolling with the waves. When Colin faced the sky, he watched the Discodactyls dive-bomb toward him one by one. Without fail, they rebounded off the clear tarp and boomeranged back toward the clouds where they continued to scan the House of Rex. Two and a half minutes later, Colin crashed into the tarp. As he pressed into the soft dome shielding the arena, his flesh flared. Like the Discodactyls, he bounced off the clear barricade, which cast him back the way he came, but before it launched him toward the dance-floor, its heat caused his body to bubble.

When the tarp had released him, "Interstellar Overdrive" climbed to its climax at a speed nearing light. As Colin's acrobatics continued, he glimpsed Emma and Velma dancing toward the middle of the mushroom's cap, trailed by Joe. The rotations of their headspins were being completed so quickly now that both of their bodies had appeared to multiply six times. The clones formed a circle around the original, creating a kaleidoscopic mirage. Across the dance-floor, Rose lunged toward the center of the cap. As he neared the wavy surface, he closed his eyes and flinched.

Three seconds after Colin had rebounded off the tarp, Rose caught him mere inches above the trough of a wave, saving him from snapping his neck. Holding him by his ankles, she spun him back and forth, loosening him up for the Grand Break. While suspended upside-down, he wondered if this would be the last time she held him in her tail. Would Rose release him if she weren't positive that she could pull this off? Behind them, Emma and Velma now performed perfect *tours en l'air* while Joe completed the triangle in front of him. However, his brother's worm had devolved to a chubby caterpillar.

As the Apatosaurus set the crown of Colin's head against the crest of a wave, he envisioned himself inside her cloaca, bathing in her fluids. But before he could dance against her warm flesh, before he could savor her liquid rainbows, Rose released him, using her tail to fling him into the fastest headspin of his life. The stands immediately morphed into a colorful mushroom cloud as the speed of his spins increased, but flashing black dots began to blot out the color. Within seconds, nausea overpowered him. It took all of his mental energy to keep himself from vomiting.

The black dots consumed Colin so that he hardly noticed his surroundings. Almost all the color had vanished, and the few small pockets that remained blinked throughout the darkness. He wondered if even these pockets would dissolve when Rose split him in half. Would he never see color again? But as he felt a sudden stab of pain around his hips, and his upper body began to rotate in the opposite direction of his legs, torrents of red fluid stained the dance-floor. Colin became a sprinkler spraying red paint across the surface of the mushroom's cap. As his torso continued to spin against his lower body, which created severe counter-nausea, he could no longer keep the vegetables down. Vomit spewed from his mouth, and he imagined he had transformed into a dragon with a brutal case of the flu.

Rose squeezed Colin's ankles with her tail, reconnecting his halves while bringing his headspin to a halt. The pain ceased. Then she flipped him onto his feet where he started an automatic two-step. Despite being upright and despite no longer spinning, the audience around him swirled as if he were stuck dancing in the center of a carousel. The nausea continued to strengthen, and he wondered if this infinite tunnel of revolving light comprised the afterlife. But before he could convince himself that the end had truly come, he regurgitated again. And after he had finished this second round of vomiting, he felt significantly more stable.

As the stands stopped dancing around Colin's eyes, silence washed over him. This lasted almost two seconds. But when the three Velociraptors held up a sign that demanded the audience **BOO**, the crowd chanted for the challengers' demise.

Rose lifted Colin onto her back and two-stepped toward their corner. As he massaged her scales, he realized strings of blood had streaked his body, as if he were a candlestick melting onto an Apatosaurus bobeche.

"Rose!" Colin shouted over the crowd. They had just reached their corner of the dance-floor. "I'm alive! I mean, we did it! We actually did the Grand Break!"

"Yeah," Rose said, curving her neck toward Colin. She planted a soft kiss on his lips and smiled weakly. "We did."

"What's wrong?" Colin asked. His whole crew seemed deflated. "We did do it, right?"

Rose nodded. Apparently, Apatosauruses can cry.

"Bau didn't come," Emma said, deadpan. "I told you all of this was crap. I told you we're fucked."

Rose just shook her head. "My whole life..." she said. "Bau's not in the sky."

The Tyrannosaurus Rex shimmied to the center of the cap,

silencing the crowd. He proclaimed, "Talk about a lame fucking dance number! Am I right?" The Velociraptors behind the table held up a sign saying **LAUGH**. The dinosaurs throughout the stands fell into fits of hysterics. Some members of the Tyrannosaurus Task Force even laughed themselves out of their seats, floating toward the clear tarp. But as the Tyrannosaurus Rex resumed his speech, they instantly brought themselves under control and sank back to the stands. "For those of you who are just waking from your naps, rest assured, you missed one of the worst challenges in dance-off history. But now that the challengers have gotten their bullshit performance over with, are you, you carnivorous studs, ready to watch the performance of an Ultimate Dinosaur Dance-Off champion?"

The crowd most definitely appeared ready.

Colin stroked the scales along Rose's back, wishing he could make her happy. Sure, Bau didn't exist, and as a consequence of her lifelong belief being false, she would now be forced to lead the Tyrannosaurus Rex and all the other carnivores back to her Astral where they would send her species to a premature extinction. Still, there had to be something he could do to cheer her up.

Before Colin could figure out the formula that would give Rose a genuine smile, Van Halen's "Jump" reverberated throughout the arena, and the Tyrannosaurus Rex pumped his puny arms. Besides nodding his head and signaling for the audience to rise to their feet, the returning champion stayed stagnant. Once the song entered its first verse, the Tyrannosaurus Rex slowly bent his knees, crouching until his butt balanced on the mushroom's cap. He remained crouched against the ground until just over a minute into the song. When "Jump" finally progressed into its chorus, the Tyrannosaurus Rex jumped as high as he could, and with the assistance of a cresting wave, he managed to leap twelve inches into the air.

When he landed back on the dance-floor, almost instantaneously after his takeoff, a toothy grin curled across his snout. He marched around the arena and flapped his feathery arms for the rest of the song. He spent most of his time patrolling the audience to make sure they were applauding him, instead of actually dancing. But each time Van Halen vocalized that the dictator jump, the Tyrannosaurus Rex leapt into the air. As the song continued, no matter how low he crouched, he failed to surpass the height of his initial attempt.

Throughout the entire performance, the crowd either roared or waved. Of course, whether they decided to **ROAR** or **WAVE** was determined by the Velociraptors' signs, which, in turn, were based off the miniscule arm maneuvers made by the Tyrannosaurus Rex as he orbited the dance-floor with his macho march. The returning champion never seemed to be disappointed with the audience's reactions, so there were no dinosaurs for the Tyrannosaurus Task Force to apprehend. As the song came to its climax, some of the Velociraptors started to fidget.

Colin still stroked Rose's scales, but he had finally figured out something to say. "What if Bau waits till after the dance-off to arrive?"

"Why would she do that?" Rose asked, sincerely.

Colin didn't have an answer. Now that he had spoken this thought out loud, it seemed stupid.

"Jump" now travelled through its closing chorus, and the Tyrannosaurus Rex leapt continuously. In addition to jumping, he had now slid his tail through his legs and angled it up across his chest. He flapped his tiny, wing-shaped arms, gently strumming his tail guitar. His boiling red head spinelessly flopped from side to side, spraying sweat all over the dance-floor as he tried to match his one-foot jump. But when the song faded away, he had yet to conquer his record. He kept jerking his head to his left, as if he were trying to shrug.

The audience erupted with admiration and applause. That's what the three Velociraptors had written on the two signs they held high: **ADMIRATION** and **APPLAUSE**. The Tyrannosaurus Rex's head grew even redder, and Colin wondered if he were blushing.

"Thank you!" The Tyrannosaurus Rex cried. "I fucking nailed it! Jump!" He jumped again. This attempt had lifted him maybe a half-foot high. "Before we discuss the feast, before we march to the Astral of the Apatosaurus, we must have a winner. Judges!" the Tyrannosaurus Rex shouted. "Have you chosen a champion?"

The Tyrannosaurus Rex didn't judge the event? Colin hoped this might even the dance-floor odds a bit. If the judges were by any means just, they would have to see the challengers were the true champions. But before his thoughts could escalate any further, the Tyrannosaurus Rex hopped over to the Velociraptors' table. Failing to lift his arm in front of his mouth to keep the rest of the creatures from reading his lips, he seemed to think a whisper would suffice. As far as Colin could tell, whispering worked perfectly.

The Tyrannosaurus Rex gleefully hopped back to the center of the cap. "The judges have declared a winner!" he cried, the excitement rising rapidly in his voice. "The champion of the three hundred and nineteenth Ultimate Dinosaur Dance-Off is—"

The sound of fabric tearing silenced the Tyrannosaurus Rex. The rainbow sky ripped in half, and all the color collapsed onto Earth. Absolute darkness covered the Days of the Dinosaur.

Colin wrapped his arms around Rose and squeezed her with all his strength. "What's happening?" he asked. His voice came across muffled, his lips pressed against the Apatosaurus's back.

"I think you were right!" Rose said.

"What do you mean?"

"I think this is Bau."

Before Colin could respond, pure light danced down from the sky in the form of a Brontosaurus. The goddess did a cosmic dance, uncoiling her neck and snapping it forward like a snake while the rest of her body rhythmically rocked from side to side. As she came closer, Colin realized the halo surrounding her had been fringed with fire, and the clear tarp covering the dance-floor evaporated under her heat. As he basked in the goddess's warmth, Atomic Forest's "Obsession '77" boomed throughout the Days of the Dinosaur.

Prehistoric Paradise Restored (Praise Bau!) (Chapter Thirty-One)

THE DISCODACTYLS ABANDONED THEIR SPOT in the sky, retreating toward their Domain as the Brontosaurus continued her descent. Bau sank toward the House of Rex until she paralleled the dinosaurs sitting in the highest seats in the stands. As she floated above the dance-floor, the goddess started stomping her hind right foot in sync with Atomic Forest's song.

Each time the Brontosaurus stomped her foot, the House of Rex shrank in increments equaling the length of an Apatosaurus's tail. And every time the mushroom's stature diminished, the surface of the cap quaked violently, as if the challengers grooved on top of two colliding tectonic plates. Colin feared death had found him. What if Bau were angry with the Apatosauruses for taking so long to summon her and now, instead of restoring paradise, she had decided to eradicate all prehistoric life? What if his dancing caused the only species he had ever wanted to love to become extinct? He felt queasy as the mushroom continued to cascade, and he wrapped his appendages around Rose's body, squeezing her so hard his muscles ached. Beside Colin and the Apatosaurus, Joe and Emma had intertwined their bodies as they sat on the cap while Velma performed a shaky two-step with her eyes securely shut.

The dinosaurs throughout the stands simply stared at the three Velociraptors in charge of the signs, unsure of how to react.

Eventually, and following the example of the Tyrannosaurus Rex, who sobbed in his corner of the dance-floor as he complained that this unfair calamity shouldn't be happening because, according to the judges, he had been unanimously voted the winner of the Ultimate Dinosaur Dance-Off, the Velociraptors raised a makeshift sign commanding the crowd to **CRY**.

Once the House of Rex had lost half of its initial height, Bau began to lift her hind left leg, causing a volcano of golden light to erupt on the other side of the island. Colin suspected the blinding brightness originated somewhere near Parrot's Point.

"What's Bau doing?" Colin asked, shouting over the song and squinting.

"I think she's restoring Prehistoric Paradise," Rose said, seemingly lost in a state of blissful bewilderment.

As the House of Rex compressed, Colin grinned. He no longer feared the Apatosaurus apocalypse. Instead, as the Brontosaurus continued to stomp the dictator's mushroom out of existence, he hugged Rose in awe, reveling in dance-off glory. He could hardly believe that his crew's performance would allow the love of his life to be free from the tyranny of the Tyrannosaurus Rex.

On the other side of the dance-floor, the dictator lay curled up on the cap as if he had never vacated his egg. As the Tyrannosaurus Rex quivered beneath Bau, his authority over the other carnivores seemed to wither in sync with the shrinking mushroom. While his sobs had become silent, fist-sized tears continued to roll down his lobster red snout, and he remained the sole dinosaur in the arena who still possessed puffy eyes.

Only the mushroom's cap remained of the House of Rex, and as Bau worked on dancing it out of history, Colin noticed the carnivores surrounding him started to evolve. The Piratops' peg legs slowly morphed into meat, the Velociraptors ceased levitating, and the Astralsauruses' eyes were perched on translucent bodies.

"What's happening to them?" Colin asked, looking over his shoulder at the now nearly opaque, feathery Astralsauruses.

"Bau must be exorcising the mystical meteor," Rose said, curving her neck so that her sight mirrored Colin's, "which is causing them to revert to their original forms. This must be what they looked like centuries ago, before the Earth danced."

Colin resisted the urge to pinch himself. Instead, he sat up on the Apatosaurus's back as he and the challengers wordlessly watched the carnivores evolve before their eyes. As the transformation continued, Colin struggled to believe how little these dinosaurs had actually mutated when the meteor shook the island over three hundred years ago. Of course, the Velociraptors no longer glowed, levitated, or smelled of cinnamon, the Astralsauruses ceased being transparent, and the Piratops had exchanged their peg legs for flesh, their parrots for horns, and their patch for an eye. But aside from these changes, their coloration and size stayed the same. The Velociraptors still possessed neon green plumage, the Deinonychuses, formerly Astralsauruses, still sported red feathers and blue beaks, and the scales of the Triceratops, formerly Piratops, remained pink and purple. Moreover, Rose hadn't changed at all. She still retained her sensuous green, purple, and blue tie-dye skin as she swayed on the shrinking cap between the island's cliff and the rainbow forest.

Bau simultaneously finished stomping the House of Rex with her right foot and lifting Prehistoric Paradise with her left. And once all the dinosaurs' adaptations had concluded and the mushroom's cap had become consumed by the Earth, Atomic Forest's "Obsession '77" came to a close. After Bau finished her dance, she immediately returned to the plane of existence from which she came, and the rainbow sky sewed itself back together.

The Zombies' "Time of the Season" started to reverberate throughout the Days of the Dinosaur, and some of the more courageous creatures sitting in the now flattened arena seats slowly began to stand. They crept away from the dance-floor, scurried up the hill, pushed past the plateau, and walked toward the light shining on the other side of the island.

Once they had moved out of view, Colin proclaimed, as if he were the only one to have witnessed this miracle, "They aren't dancing!"

"Of course they aren't fucking dancing," wailed the Tyrannosaurus Rex. "You won the Ultimate Dinosaur Dance-Off. The time of Tuque is done. The Meteor of Mystical Movement has been vanquished."

Hearing the cry of the Tyrannosaurus Rex, the dinosaurs who still resided in the stands promptly rose and retreated up the hill in the direction of their friends. Velma left the rest of the challengers to follow them. Holding hands, Joe and Emma took a tentative step toward the incline, as if they were trying to prove to themselves that they could indeed walk again. They succeeded, and taking one slow step after another, they walked toward the base of the hill. Colin asked Rose if she would set him down so he could try walking, too. And together, he and the Apatosaurus sauntered in circles. When Joe and Emma reached the base of the hill, they turned around and strode back toward the rest of the challengers.

"Is it really over?" Joe asked dreamily.

"Can we go home?" Emma added, hopeful.

"Are you blind?" the Tyrannosaurus Rex cried, sounding as if he had been celery-slapped in the face. "Can you not see that all my friends have forsaken me? And for what? To live life in a paradise where we cannot even enjoy the freedom of a leafless meal?" Slowly, the Tyrannosaurus Rex rose to his feet. "'Is it really over?'" he mimicked, flailing his winged-arms. "Of course it's over. This is your Prehistoric Paradise restored." Drooping, he trudged toward the hill and, after a tedious climb, disappeared.

Colin had nearly forgotten about going home. While the question of whether or not he would be forced to leave Rose after freeing her species had certainly been looming in the back of his mind, he had worked hard to keep it from fully materializing. But now he had no choice. Would he be forced to leave? Would Rose become nothing more than a prehistoric trophy trapped in a museum?

"Yes," Rose said, smiling faintly. "All you have to do is walk along the River of Rex until you reach the light. The Apatosauruses will be waiting for you with a reconstructed Brontosaurus pirate ship that will take you home."

"But do we..." Colin cleared his throat. "Can we not stay in Prehistoric Paradise?"

Rose leaned over Colin and softly kissed the top of his head while she slid her tail into his hands. "The Apatosauruses would never allow alien dancers from the future to stay in their paradise. They've waited too long and have fought too hard to regain the paradise they lost, and now that they've attained it, the risk of allowing you to stay is too great. Being from the future, your very existence is a threat to the paradise of prehistory."

Colin felt numb, like he had been buried beneath the cold droppings of the Discodactyls. He couldn't go home. Now that he had experienced life with a living Apatosaurus, he could never go back to fossils and paleoart. He wanted to sprint to the cliffside and dive into the sea, but he couldn't bring his muscles into motion.

"That doesn't make any sense," Joe complained. "Prehistoric times are already full of the future. How could Colin's presence make a difference?"

Rose nodded. "It's strange," she said. "My whole life I dreamed of paradise. I thought if the right aliens would just dance through time and fix our society, everything would be perfect." She pulled her tail out of Colin's hands and snuggly wrapped it around his body. "But I never thought one of your kind could affect me like this. Our saviors were supposed to be nothing more than fond memories in every dinosaur's mind. You were never meant to be more than a cherished relic from the distant future."

"But why does that make him such a colossal threat to dinosaur society?" Emma asked. Her forehead scrunched.

"Because I can no longer live in a paradise where dinosaurs aren't allowed to mate singularly whenever they wish."

Colin pinched his tongue with his teeth. Did this mean Rose wanted to mate solely with him? Despite the pain in his mouth, he struggled seeing this as anything but a dream.

"I can no longer live in a paradise that will inevitably fall to the dominance of DinoMania," Rose continued. "Don't you see that DinoMania hatches when a dinosaur values a mate over every other living creature? Don't you see that forcing all dinosaurs to mate with as many creatures as possible doesn't do anything to prevent a dinosaur from becoming DinoManic when they accidentally fall in love? Don't you see that even in Prehistoric Paradise, dinosaurs fall in love? Tuque did, and it's just a matter of time before another dinosaur does. In Prehistoric Paradise, they don't see this. They don't understand that paradise only suppresses DinoMania, and eventually, creates it. They don't see that to truly defeat DinoMania, a dinosaur must be able to maintain a singular mate while simultaneously refusing to value said mate over any other dinosaur."

Joe and Emma, who had not heard of DinoMania until now, looked entirely lost. Even with his limited understanding of the condition and its relationship to dinosaur society, Colin didn't really know what Rose meant. Instead of further complicating the matter by asking for a second explanation, he simply said, "Is there not another way I can stay?"

"There is," Rose said, looking at her feet. "But would you be willing to take the risk that it would require?"

"I'd do anything."

Rose grinned and squeezed him three times with her tail. "We can leave the island."

"Where will we go?" Colin asked, captivated.

Rose pointed her neck toward the cliffside and to the sea beyond.

"Have other dinosaurs left the island before?" Colin asked.

Rose shook her head. "Never," she said. "Our ancestors believed that there was nothing waiting out there. They taught us that if we were to leave, the sea would swallow us. But I've always thought there had to be more land. And, well, if I'm wrong, at least we'll be together for the remainder of our lives."

"You're not wrong," Joe said. "At least, there's more land where we're from, and it couldn't have come from nowhere."

"There will be land," Colin agreed, confident. "And together, we'll find a new island, a bigger island, where we can mate freely and forever."

"But where does that leave us?" Emma asked, blushing.

"What do you mean?" Colin asked.

"Well, aren't there supposed to be three humans? Will Reggie and the rest of the Apatosauruses actually let us leave the island if we return without you and Rose?"

"They will if they think we're dead," Rose said.

"Okay," Emma said, "sure. But why would they believe us? I mean, there will be plenty of dinosaurs in paradise who witnessed your performance in the dance-off, so your death has to have happened sometime between Bau's ascent and our return, which seems highly unlikely since paradise has just been restored."

"Say that you're Colin," Rose said, pointing her neck at Joe, "and that your captured friend succumbed to sickness. Tell them that Joe infected me with his human disease, and that I died shortly after the dance-off on our trek across the island, which is why it took you so much longer than the other dinosaurs to reach Prehistoric Paradise."

"And that will actually work?" Joe asked.

"I think so," Rose said, unraveling her tail, releasing Colin. "They won't leave the heart of paradise to dispose of my infected carcass. But even if for some reason they do, you'll be long gone by the time they discover there is no body."

Emma and Joe nodded. Colin hugged his brother and his friend and told them that he'd never forget them and what they had done to preserve dinosaurkind. When The Zombies' song concluded, and silence had washed over them, he ended their embrace and walked back to Rose's tail. She coiled it around him and lifted him onto her back. Colin waved to the last of his species he would ever see as they started to retreat along the River of Rex toward the light and the lagoon. He kept waving until Rose leapt over the edge of the cliff, causing his stomach to spring out of his body.

As they fell through the air, Colin wrapped his arms around Rose's neck and clung to her as he closed his eyes and screamed. They crashed into the water and continued to fall, and Colin started to worry about Rose's ability to swim. But before he could convince himself that they were going to drown, that a dinosaur as large as Rose couldn't possibly float, they popped up over the surface, like a hatching dinosaur emerging from the egg.

Colin let go of Rose's neck and rested on her back. As he lay there soaking in the sun, The Lovin' Spoonful's "Daydream" began to float above the wavy water. Surrounded by the sea, Colin suddenly realized how intense his thirst had already become. He hoped he and Rose would find an island soon, hoped that the island would have an infinite supply of fresh water, but the endless expanse of ocean enveloped his vision. The Apatosaurus continued to swim west. In the distance, the rainbow sun began to sink below the horizon, turning the water around them into a forest of vibrant color.

Acknowledgments

I owe a great deal of thanks to the following people:

Nicholas Day, Don Noble, and everyone at JournalStone for taking a chance on this book. Everyone in the CalArts Creative Writing MFA program in 2016. My mentors at CalArts, Brian Evenson and Jon Wagner, who provided me with invaluable feedback on this manuscript as it went through various drafts. And CalArts itself for allowing and encouraging me to work on this ridiculous novel as my graduate thesis (and for buying me an inflatable dinosaur costume for my graduate reading). Brendan Vidito, Laura Lee Bahr, Andrew Goldfarb, Diego Cepeda, Char Simpson, Shane Cartledge, Zé Burns, Katy Michelle Quinn, Jake Edgar, and Brian Allen Carr for their excitement about this project and their continued support of my work. My family and my children for inspiring and encouraging me. And finally thank you from the bottom of my heart to anyone who has ever read my work.

Moreover, the idea for this book would have never existed if it weren't for Alice's Adventures in Wonderland and The Land Before Time, both of which have deeply influenced me since childhood.

List of Songs Found Within *The Ultimate Dinosaur Dance-Off*:

1. "Cosmic Dancer" by T. Rex
2. "U Can't Touch This" by MC Hammer
3. "Brontosaurus" by The Move
4. "Love Buzz" by Shocking Blue
5. "We Can Be Together" by Jefferson Airplane
6. "Let's Get It On" by Marvin Gaye
7. "Are You Ready" by The Chambers Brothers
8. "Tequila" by The Champs
9. "Strange Days" by The Doors
10. "Dance To The Medley" by Sly & The Family Stone
11. "Astral Plane" by The Modern Lovers
12. "Nights in White Satin" by The Moody Blues
13. "Fire" by The Crazy World of Arthur Brown
14. "Dimension" by Wolfmother
15. "It's A Beautiful Day Today" by Moby Grape
16. "(Ballad Of) The Hip Death Goddess" by Ultimate Spinach
17. "Going Up The Country" by Canned Heat
18. "Fresh Air" by Quicksilver Messenger Service
19. "She's A Rainbow" by The Rolling Stones
20. "Funkytown" by Lipps Inc
21. "The Garden Of Earthly Delights" by The United States of America
22. "Friggin' In The Riggin'" by Sex Pistols
23. "Incense And Peppermints" by Strawberry Alarm Clock
24. "Oaxaca" by Froth
25. "Crosstown Traffic" by The Jimi Hendrix Experience
26. "Lucy In The Sky With Diamonds" by The Beatles
27. "Sunshine Of Your Love" by Cream
28. "Red Rubber Ball" by The Cyrkle
29. "The Golden Road [To Unlimited Devotion]" by Grateful Dead
30. "Hey Ya!" by OutKast
31. "We Gotta Get Out Of This Place" by The Animals
32. "You're Gonna Miss Me" by The 13th Floor Elevators
33. "California Dreamin'" by The Mamas & The Papas
34. "You Can't Win" by Iron Butterfly
35. "Bad Moon Rising" by Creedence Clearwater Revival
36. "Get The Funk Out Ma Face" by The Brothers Johnson
37. "Walk The Dinosaur" by Was (Not Was)
38. "Whole Lotta Love" by Led Zeppelin
39. "Gloria" by The Shadows of Knight
40. "She Comes In Colors" by Love
41. "Loser" by Beck
42. "We Will Rock You" by Queen
43. "Let's Dance" by David Bowie
44. "Interstellar Overdrive" by Pink Floyd
45. "Jump" by Van Halen
46. "Obsession '77 (Fast)" by Atomic Forest
47. "Time Of The Season" by The Zombies
48. "Daydream" by The Lovin' Spoonful

About the Author

(photo courtesy of Sam Reeve)

If Andrew J. Stone were a dinosaur, he'd be an Apatosaurus. If he were a superhero, he'd be Marx. If he were to have a cat, her name would be Alice, and he'd be living in a residence that allowed pets. He is the author of the novellas *The Mortuary Monster* and *All Hail the House Gods*, both from Strangehouse Books. His short stories have appeared in Hobart, New Dead Families, Drunk Monkeys, and DOGZPLOT, among other places. His work has been translated into Spanish by the Colombian publisher Ediciones Vestigio. He lives in Manhattan Beach, California with his wife, their twins, and his in-laws.